How I Beat Coca-Cola and Other Tales of One-Upmanship

Books by the Same Author

Fiction

Cantor's Dilemma
The Bourbaki Gambit
Marx, Deceased
Menachem's Seed
NO

Poetry

The Clock Runs Backward
A Diary of Pique

Drama

An Immaculate Misconception: Sex in an Age of Mechanical Reproduction
Oxygen (with Roald Hoffmann)
Calculus
Ego: Three on a Couch
Phallacy
Sex in an Age of Technological Reproduction: ICSI and TABOOS
Foreplay: Hannah Arendt, the Two Adornos, and Walter Benjamin
Insufficiency
NO (a pedagogic wordplay, with Pierre Laszlo)

Nonfiction

The Politics of Contraception
Steroids Made It Possible (scientific autobiography)
The Pill, Pygmy Chimps, and Degas' Horse: The Autobiography of Carl Djerassi
From the Lab into the World: A Pill for People, Pets, and Bugs
This Man's Pill: Reflections on the 50th Birthday of the Pill (memoir)
Four Jews on Parnassus—A Conversation: Benjamin, Adorno, Scholem, Schönberg
Chemistry in Theatre: Insufficiency, Phallacy or Both

Scientific Monographs

Optical Rotatory Dispersion: Applications to Organic Chemistry
Steroid Reactions: An Outline for Organic Chemists (editor)
Interpretation of Mass Spectra of Organic Compounds
(with H. Budzikiewicz and D. H. Williams)
Structure Elucidation of Natural Products by Mass Spectrometry
(2 volumes with H. Budzikiewicz and D. H. Williams)
Mass Spectrometry of Organic Compounds
(with H. Budzikiewicz and D. H. Williams)

How I Beat Coca-Cola and Other Tales of One-Upmanship

Carl Djerassi

Terrace Books
A trade imprint of the University of Wisconsin Press

Terrace Books, a trade imprint of the University of Wisconsin Press, takes its name from the Memorial Union Terrace, located at the University of Wisconsin–Madison. Since its inception in 1907, the Wisconsin Union has provided a venue for students, faculty, staff, and alumni to debate art, music, politics, and the issues of the day. It is a place where theater, music, drama, literature, dance, outdoor activities, and major speakers are made available to the campus and the community. To learn more about the Union, visit www.union.wisc.edu.

Terrace Books
A trade imprint of the University of Wisconsin Press
1930 Monroe Street, 3rd Floor
Madison, Wisconsin 53711-2059
uwpress.wisc.edu

3 Henrietta Street
London WC2E 8LU, England
eurospanbookstore.com

Printed in the United States of America

Library of Congress Cataloging-in-Publication Data
Djerassi, Carl.
[Short stories. Selections]
How I beat Coca-Cola and other tales of one-upmanship / Carl Djerassi.
p. cm.
ISBN 978-0-299-29504-2 (pbk.: alk. paper)
ISBN 978-0-299-29503-5 (e-book)
I. Title.
PS3554.J47H69 2013
813'.54—dc23
2013010471

Each person completely touches us
With what he is and as he is,
In the stale grandeur of annihilation.

Wallace Stevens, *Lebensweisheitspielerei*

Contents

Preface

Why burden a collection of seemingly disparate short stories with a preface? Everyone knows that short stories are often finger exercises in preparation for a full concert. The first piece of fiction I ever wrote, the short story "Castor's Dilemma," did indeed represent such a finger exercise as a prelude to my first "science-in-fiction" novel, *Cantor's Dilemma*. But my motivation for writing twelve variations around the common theme of one-upmanship does warrant a brief explanation.

The scientist behind my literary persona drives me all too frequently toward drawing an accurate picture of the contemporary science scene through the medium of realistic fiction—at times so realistic as to border on literary journalism or on autobiography. But fiction authors are frequently autobiographers wearing a mask; I admit openly and indeed proudly that this statement applies to me. Why proudly? Because scientific researchers, notably those on the harder edges of chemistry and physics, are members of a tribal culture whose behavioral idiosyncrasies are not only unfamiliar to the outside world but frequently are not even recognized by members of the tribe. Knowledge of how to behave as a scientist—indeed what it means to be a scientist—is generally not taught in courses or books, but is acquired through a long osmotic process during the traditional mentor-disciple relationship. Gradually we accept the white laboratory coat as our cultural uniform.

Having conducted chemical research for nearly half a century, I certainly qualify as a member of the species *Homo scientificus*. Whether that also qualifies me to write effectively about the cultural practices of our tribe is a judgment that only the reader can render, although I shall make the case that it takes an insider to illuminate some of our more esoteric cultural practices covering the range from exceptionally generous collegiality all the way to brutally competitive Nobel lust, with my story "Castor's Dilemma" illustrating that point. The overwhelming majority of working scientists spend little time on introspection and self-analysis. We are trained to analyze the world around us in exquisite detail and often with amazing insight, but very seldom do we apply these skills to an examination of our tribal behavior. I was not very different in that respect until my early sixties when I decided upon a form of auto-psychoanalysis through writing in the genre of "science-in-fiction" that allowed me a freedom of expression that shame, embarrassment, or even fear might have prevented me to use in the form of conventional nonfiction.

One-upmanship—trumping competitors and colleagues alike—is endemic among research scientists. Winning an argument is crucial—as is the accompanying admiration and envy it engenders. But even brief reflection will show that it is in fact a human foible that can be found wherever one searches for it. And since I have practiced one-upmanship for most of my adult life—often to my detriment—I thought that the most painless way of confessing that character fault of mine—still in full bloom on my ninetieth birthday—is in the guise of fiction and in areas that have always appealed to me: food ("Noblesse Oblige"), sex ("What's Tatiana Troyanos Doing in Spartacus's Tent?"), art ("The Futurist"), opera ("The Glyndebourne Heist"), human companionship ("Maskenfreiheit"), word play ("The Toyota Cantos"), and, of course, science ("How I Beat Coca-Cola" and "The Dacriologist"). Even the choice of some of the titles (e.g., "The Psomophile") is a manifestation of one-upmanship, although the ultimate confirmation of its success will only arrive when the Oxford English Dictionary or Webster's enters this invented word of mine in its next edition. Much of what I tell in these twelve short stories is autobiographical, though very little of it is biographical: it didn't happen to me as told, but it could have. To that extent, it is much more honest than conventional autobiography, which itself is a form of automythological fiction in which I have also indulged in the past.

The short story was the medium through which I first entered into literature after decades as a chemist in industry and academia, to then proceed writing novels and finally plays. During the past quarter century, this collection of short stories has been published in half a dozen countries, but never in the United States. Although my mother tongue is German, my literary writing is entirely in English, the only language in which I am truly comfortable since my immigration to the United States as a teenage refugee from Vienna. After five novels and nine plays, to finally see my very first literary endeavor appear in the United States through the press of the university where I received my training as a chemist seventy years ago is a memorable way to celebrate my ninetieth birthday.

How I Beat Coca-Cola and Other Tales of One-Upmanship

How I Beat Coca-Cola

Actually, it wasn't all that difficult, once they realized I was serious and not about to bargain. "Please sir," I said quietly, holding up my hand. "Please. This isn't a bazaar, or one of your union bargaining sessions." (This was a gaffe; at this stage I didn't know that Coca-Cola has no union.) "If you consider what's at stake here, I'm asking for something quite modest: twenty-five per annum, after taxes . . . for life, of course." Initially, I hadn't thought about the tax angle, but when he started haggling, I knew I had him hooked. "Modest?" he sputtered, his face turning the same color as litmus when dipped into acid. "You can't be older than thirty . . ."—"Thirty-one," I interrupted—"and you may easily live another fifty years . . ." "Easily," I agreed. "My grandfather is ninety-six and still takes a walk to the park every day. My father is sixty-one, and still plays a mean game of tennis." "*Modest!*" he repeated himself. "Son, that's one and a quarter *billion*. If taxes stay where they're now, that's . . ." (he opened the desk drawer and punched a few keys on his calculator) "$41,344,945 annual gross income. And I haven't even added your self-employment tax, whatever that amounts to." "Don't forget state taxes," I said, but then took pity. "Sir," I continued, figuring I could afford to act deferential, because once

Coca-Cola signed on the dotted line, he'd be "Doug" and I'd be "Russ."
"Forty-one *million* plus some change per year is a bagatelle for a corporation the size of yours." (I've never used the word "bagatelle" before, but the way it popped out, it must have been waiting in my subconscious for just such an occasion. I thought it was rather apt: elegant, with just the right touch of flippancy—a real bon mot for forty-one million *before* taxes. I was also pleased that the word "dollars" never crossed my lips.)

But I'm getting ahead of myself. You wanted to know how it all started. It was in sixth grade, at a science fair. At that time I didn't give beans for science. Soccer was all that interested me. That, and Coke. Coke for breakfast, Coke for lunch, Coke before soccer, several Cokes after the game, Coke at supper . . . "Russ, honey," my mother used to worry, "all that Coke isn't healthy for a growing boy. No wonder you aren't big enough for football. You need *milk* for your bones. Think what all that phosphoric acid will do to the lining of your stomach."
"Mother," I replied in a tone that only a pained youth who knows better can muster, "phosphoric acid! Puh-leeze!"

But at that fair, a kid in my class performed an experiment that changed my life, and at the same time bound me permanently to Coke. Of course, I didn't know that then. In fact, initially I was rather pissed off by the whole affair. The kid won first prize, but it should've been obvious to everyone—especially the judge—that the experiment couldn't have been his idea. Later on, I found out that I was right: his father, a chemist in some drug company, had thought of it and even provided the equipment. How many sixth graders have a distillation apparatus with a fancy, coiled condenser, fitted glass joints (no corks or rubber stoppers for this budding chemistry genius), and an electric heating mantle? He even had a powerstat from which the father had not bothered to remove the inventory label bearing the name of the drug company. How do I remember all this? Because in the end, I became so fascinated by the experiment that I went back to help the kid take it all apart after he'd won first prize.

It was really quite simple. The kid took some coffee from a thermos (I bet his mother brewed it), asked the judge to taste it ("Yes," the hypocrite nodded, feigning interest, "delicious coffee, but what now?"), and then poured it into the distillation flask. He attached the distillation head and condenser, ran cold water from a nearby faucet through the condenser coils, turned the powerstat to its highest setting, and sat down, looking smug. After a few minutes, the coffee started to boil; pretty soon, a colorless liquid dripped out at the other end of the condenser. "Behold the distillate in the Erlenmeyer," he pontificated, as he swirled the flask at the other end of the condenser. Can you imagine a kid saying "behold"? Or "Erlenmeyer"? I bet he didn't even know how to spell it.

Next to his set-up, he had two cups and saucers (with the type of curlicue design I hate), sugar bowl and creamer (with matching curlicues, of course), and two all-too-precious embossed spoons—the type aunts give to infant nephews. The kid's mother must have made at least six cups of coffee. When about half of that had distilled over into the Erlenmeyer flask (to this day, I—a Ph.D. in analytical chemistry—think of that sixth grade scene every time I pick up an Erlenmeyer in the lab), he poured some of the colorless distillate into one cup and filled the other with the black liquid remaining in the original round-bottomed distillation flask. "How would you like your coffee, ma'am?" he asked the judge. "Sugar? Cream? Or just . . . ?" "Just black," the judge replied, reaching for the second cup with the coffee-colored liquid. She grimaced as she took a sip. "Perhaps you'd like your coffee colorless," the clever little jerk suggested, proffering the cup containing some of the transparent distillate. His expression was so smug that I was tempted to knock the cup out of his hand, but it was too late. The woman hadn't even taken one sip—she had just sniffed it gingerly—and I could tell instantly that he'd won first prize. "My goodness!" she exclaimed.

He reached under the table to produce a very professional chart—not written or typed, but printed in some special font (most likely by his father's audiovisual department). In concise language, it summarized the lesson we were all supposed to have learned: what you can smell—in this instance the aroma of coffee—must, by definition, be volatile. The residual black color is just a psychological cue without taste or smell, with the caffeine providing the physiological kick. All the volatile constituents had passed over into the Erlenmeyer flask during the distillation process, leaving behind coffee-colored nothingness.

"What's the aroma made out of?" I asked the chemist father when I helped in the disassembly. "It's too complicated," he muttered. "You wouldn't understand." Even then I sensed that the respondent didn't know either.

What's that got to do with Coke? I'm getting to it. Six years later, as a freshman in college, I had to take two semesters of science. I had biology but not chemistry in high school, and I figured that biology would be easier. Even as a freshman, I was sure I'd go into biz ad, so I wanted to get my science requirement out of the way in the quickest and most painless way. But I'd fallen for a buxom, freckled redhead, who also had brains and had decided to become a second Madame Curie. So I followed her into freshman chemistry and got hooked. The instructor was young and, as the Brits say, keen. In addition he was patient and a first-class teacher. When we did our first experiments in the lab and started on distillation, I recalled the coffee episode and repeated my question of six years ago. "Extremely complicated, Russell," he started. "By now, chemists have isolated and identified over five-hundred volatile constituents from coffee. Of course, not all of them contribute to the characteristic aroma or taste of coffee." And then he rattled off a dozen or more chemical names. At that time, all I heard were some of the acids: acetic, propionic, butyric. . . . But even then one name stuck in my freshman chemist's mind: furfuryl mercaptan. "*Mercaptan?*" I gasped. "But mercaptans stink! How come they are in coffee?"

One reason Dr. Brauman was such a superb teacher was that he embellished seemingly dull chemical topics with intriguing and relevant commentary. ("Cool" is how I described it as a freshman). When he first lectured on mercaptans—a class of organic sulfur compounds—he brought up isoamyl and crotyl mercaptans, the ingredients responsible for the protective stench of skunks.

"Many mercaptans stink, but it also depends on the amount and what they are mixed with. A couple of drops of furfuryl mercaptan will make a pint of water smell like a very passable cup of coffee. It's formed during the roasting process from sugars present in the coffee bean." "But how did they identify all these compounds?" I asked. "Do you *really* want to know?" I just nodded, whereupon he pointed me down the path I'm still following. "Take second-year chemistry. That's when you'll start to learn about modern analytical chemistry: sophisticated separation methods like GC, TLC, HPLC; sensitive detection and characterization methodology like MS and NMR. That's why we can now detect parts per billion of most chemicals, when just a couple of decades ago we were lucky to do it with a few parts per million." "GC, TLC, HPLC, MS, NMR?" I echoed. Now you can wake me up at three in the morning and I will mutter the information Dr. Brauman gave me then: "gas chromatography, thin-layer chromatography, high-performance liquid chromatography, mass spectrometry, nuclear magnetic resonance."

I'll skip to the Coca-Cola Company. As an eighth-grade graduation gift, my grandfather gave me one hundred shares of Coca-Cola common stock. "If you drink that much Coke, you might as well benefit from their profits." When I graduated from high school, he presented me with another hundred shares, pointing out that during my four years in high school my original eighth-grade Coca-Cola shares had appreciated by a couple of hundred percent. My grandfather, who had only recently retired from forty-five years of practice as a patent attorney, has a marvelous face: tanned (from all that walking), with wrinkles around the eyes and mouth that only decades of good humor can etch, and eyes that always focus on yours. "The real secret of Coke's success," he said, leaning forward to look me even closer in the face, "is how they capitalize on Coke's essence, the syrup containing all the flavor and aroma that get kids like you hooked for life. The syrup John Pemberton, a pharmacist in Atlanta, had formulated in 1886." (And then he digressed: did I know that in 1935, the Orthodox Rabbi Tobias Geffen of Atlanta had convinced the almighty Coca-Cola Company to change one of its animal-derived ingredients to make Coke kosher and acceptable for Passover?) "But instead of patenting the syrup, they decided to keep it a tightly held trade secret. Why? Because if you patent something, you've got to publish the details in your patent application. In return for divulging the proprietary information to the public, the government gives you a limited monopoly on your invention, no more than twenty years. But after that, anybody can use it. Coke wanted to maintain their monopoly for much longer—forever, it seems—so they opted for the open-ended, but also much riskier, trade-secret route."

I asked the obvious question: "Then why does anybody patent an invention? Why don't they all treat them as trade secrets? Like Coke."

"Ah," my grandfather smiled, "and where would that leave us patent lawyers, Russ? Fortunately for us, if people did that, and really kept their inventions from everybody," he leaned forward again and poked me with his right index finger in the chest until it hurt, "somebody else could come along, rediscover that secret, patent it, and then keep the *original* inventor from practicing his own discovery. Or else, demand a license or royalty."

Nine years after my high school graduation, I received my Ph.D. in analytical chemistry and sold all of my shares in Coke—a lot more than the original two hundred shares, considering all the intervening stock splits. I made a handsome profit, though peanuts compared to what I needed. But my grandfather staked me to the rest to allow me to set up a smallish state-of-the-art analytical lab in the university town where I'd gotten my degree. This way, I figured, I'd have access to the chemistry department library and to some of the really expensive equipment—the high-field nuclear magnetic resonance spectrometer or the double-focusing, high-resolution mass spectrometer—I'd need on occasion but couldn't afford. (Those two instruments alone would have set us back well over a million bucks).

It took longer than I expected—nearly four years—but my grandfather didn't lose faith. We'd structured it as an arm's-length business deal: the initial losses would all be tax-deductible for my grandfather, and the eventual profits from my patent would first be used to pay off the loans with interest at prime plus 2 percent before I would collect a dime. I realized, of course, that the business arrangement was a bit of a charade, since I was his principal heir. My grandfather was in his nineties and quite well off. What would he do with all that extra money in the event I succeeded? Still, we felt that the principle of a loan, rather than an outright gift, was preferable from a tax standpoint.

I've never calculated how much Coke I bought during those four years—now mostly for purposes of concentration and experimentation rather than personal consumption. But finally I cracked it. I unveiled my chemical treasure in my grandfather's home, with my parents and my paternal grandparents sitting around the dinner table, which was covered with their best starched linen tablecloth. The table bore twenty-four crystal wineglasses that had never been used before. I had purchased them the preceding day—each numbered on the under-surface. I brought in twelve cans of Classic Coke and a crystal decanter of my own RR. Originally, RR was my grandfather's code for "Russell's Recipe," but one day I called it Roca-Rola and the name stuck. It seemed rather apposite for the nineties; and when my grandfather discovered to his amazement that the Coca-Cola Company had not protected such a closely related name, we registered it as a trademark with the U.S. Patent Office, "just in case." The trademark, of course, would mean nothing without the chemical patent application based on my four years work—an application that the U.S. Patent Office had just allowed. We had exactly three months before the actual patent would be issued and published.

My grandfather opened the twelve cans and had everyone note the numbers of the glasses—1 to 12—into which he poured the partial contents of each Coke can. The glasses numbered 13 to 24 were filled with Roca-Rola. All but my grandmother left the room, whereupon she rearranged the twenty-four filled glasses in random order. Once done, she came out, and my mother entered to repeat the scrambling of the glasses; then my father did, and, finally, my grandfather. Then came the tasting, which was, for me, a forgone conclusion. I had tasted too many Cokes and Roca-Rolas during the past six months to have any doubt that my genetic progenitors would be unable to differentiate any of the twenty-four glasses. And why should they? Even the most sophisticated chemical analyses had shown that all 227 constituents of Classic Coke were present in identical amounts in RR.

In the end, the toughest part was getting to see Coca-Cola's CEO. I had slightly less than three months to convince the company of the legal validity of my discovery and of the reasonableness of the financial bagatelle. If they accepted the latter, I would squelch the issuance of my patent and agree to keep Coke's secret. If they did not agree—or worse, if I could not even demonstrate to Coca-Cola's CEO and their board of directors that I was not a kook—I would allow my patent to be issued. But this way was likely to be a Pyrrhic patent victory. Coca-Cola could probably bleed me to death in the protracted legal battle, before I would be able to enforce my patent rights.

Did I hire an army of lawyers? Not an army, but rather P. S. Blight, Esquire. Young and subtly aggressive, my attorney was a believer in the straightforward approach. "Make it simple, and don't tip your financial hand. Enclose a certified copy of the allowed patent application. Offer to demonstrate the results to *one* company chemist (provided he is accompanied by the CEO), and mail it all by Federal Express, marked *Private and Confidential*." The simplicity of this advice appealed to me and in a couple of days the package was sent under the name and address of "P. S. Blight, Esq." to the CEO at One Coca-Cola Plaza in Atlanta, Georgia 30313. We thought the initial "P." would be better than the full name. After all, "Pandora S. Blight" might trigger some wrong subconscious buttons. Pandora is also my wife (I didn't marry the redhead who led me into chemistry), and I figured they would meet her soon enough if everything went according to plan; for it was she who had come up with the ultimate financial strategy.

In retrospect, enclosure of the patent application with the Patent Office Allowance attached to it—right in the first Federal Express missive—did the trick. The application contained so many precise, technical details that any chemical expert would have to take it seriously. When the chief chemist's secretary telephoned, I stopped her cold. "I cannot deal with surrogates," I said politely, but firmly. "The issue at hand is too sensitive." When I heard the man's voice, I started immediately in chemist-to-chemist fashion: "We're prepared to offer experimental verification in the lab for all the claims made in the patent." I didn't let on that I was the entire scientific staff. I didn't have to lie; we chemists, like politicians, always use the royal we, and I was extra careful to use only the first person plural. So one Friday morning, Coca-Cola's chief chemist and CEO appeared in my lab. The way they looked around told me they were impressed, but then every chemist can recognize a first-class lab when he sees one. I had purposely not cleared the lab benches. Quite the contrary. All the stuff I left lying around—the blinking lights, the smooth purr of the extraction fan in the stainless steel hood, the rotary evaporator swirling around slowly as if the two visitors had just interrupted me in some evaporation step, the automatic fraction collector of the computer-controlled HPLC clicking every time a new collection tube moved into position—all indicated high-tech science. I wore my lab coat, safety glasses, and plastic gloves, which I took off to shake their hands. I even offered each of them a pair of safety glasses—"You know," I smiled collegially at the chemist, "standard procedure." I have no separate office (there was no need to increase overhead) so I had pulled up chairs to my desk, which was covered in properly chaotic fashion with lab notebook, chromatography printouts, and some spectra. The CEO in his blue pinstripe suit looked uncomfortable in the bulky safety glasses with their side shields. I had given a great deal of thought to this first encounter. "Gentlemen," I said, "let me get straight to the point." Again, except for some special lab touches like the safety glasses and the beakers, I decided to follow Pandora's dictum—make it simple and straightforward. And I planned to be very formal. I was hoping that the formality and my beard would compensate at least partially for my apparent youth.

I rose and returned with four clean 250 mL beakers, which I put right on top of the spectra on my desk. No cut crystal and linen for this occasion: I wanted it to be strictly techie, from alpha to omega. From the refrigerator I fetched one can of Classic Coke and a stoppered Erlenmeyer flask bearing the carefully printed, bold label: *Roca-Rola Synth.* They said nothing—not even small talk, which I took to be a good sign. I pushed two of the beakers in the CEO's direction, filling one with Coke and the other with RR. I repeated the process for the chemist, punctuating it with just the faintest bow. "See whether you can tell them apart." I have to admit that they kept their facial expressions completely under control. The CEO took a few sips from the first beaker, then the second. He repeated the process a couple more times, then sat back and gave his chief chemist a long, unblinking look. It may have been a prearranged cue, because the man didn't even beat around the bush. "But how do we know where"—he stopped, not hiding a grimace while pointing to the Erlenmeyer—"your so-called Roca-Rola comes from." "Of course," I said quickly. "I'll make a new batch in front of you, provided you sign this nondisclosure agreement." Pandora had told me that such agreements are standard procedure when confidential information is exchanged among corporations and that the executives would not be put off by it—indeed they would expect such a demand. After reading the two-page document, the chemist handed it over to the CEO, who took a bit more time to finish it. But then he reached into his inside pocket, produced a fat Mont Blanc fountain pen, and signed on the dotted line. The chief chemist followed suit, adding today's date that the CEO and I had overlooked. "It will take close to six hours," I informed them. "When would you like me to do this?" Then the CEO took me by surprise. "Now," he replied. "In front of us."

I had not expected to demonstrate a Coca-Cola reincarnation that very day, but in the end my obvious lack of preparation gave the whole procedure an extra dose of authenticity. I did, of course, have all 227 constituent chemicals; in fact, I had many more in the lab, but originally I had intended to stage quite a performance: I had planned to arrange numerically all 227 bottles in my reagent cupboard, their order of addition and precise amounts typed out neatly on a few sheets of paper. Now, I found myself searching for a bottle here and another there, frequently referring to my lab notebook. A few milliliters of each bottle was transferred to 227 containers of a Rube Goldberg apparatus that I had constructed out of an automatic pipetting machine controlled by a small computer. I wanted to demonstrate that my Roca-Rola process could easily be automated. I was nervous, but as I look back on those hours, stretching into the middle afternoon without a break for lunch or coffee, I can see how persuasive the operation must have appeared to these two suspicious inspectors.

One bit of conversation, inspired by the impromptu nature of the performance, seemed especially impressive. I had prepared two and one-half liters of Roca-Rola. As I poured exactly two liters into a pressure bottle, connected it to a small carbon dioxide cylinder, and carefully measured by means of a flowmeter the amount of administered gas, I bantered over my shoulder, "You do know how much CO_2 a can of Coke contains?" Though workers in a bottling plant might know about such carbonation minutiae, I was convinced that no chief chemist or CEO of a multibillion-dollar corporation was likely to have such trivia at his fingertips. I turned around as if surprised. "You don't?" I proceeded to tell them, not bothering to mention that this was a minor piece of gas analysis I had performed only a month or so ago, because I could afford to leave it to the very end. Coke's myth—now the subject of my patent—is the syrup, not the gas.

I put the pressure bottle in the freezer. "Let's cool it for a few minutes," I said. "The pause that refreshes tastes better cold." To make up for this corny cuteness which came out rather flat, I added, "By the way, the men's room is just down the corridor, second door on the right." We had not even taken a toilet break. They accepted my offer, one at a time. I didn't blame them for not wanting me to remain alone in the lab for even a few minutes. I would have done the same if someone had proposed to extract a billion-plus dollars from my corporate pocket.

There isn't much more to tell. The laboratory demonstration led to the *mano a mano* tussle in the CEO's office I have already described. Tussle may be too strong a word, because it was obvious that I had won. The question was only the price for the total obliteration of my impending patent and for the assignment of the Roca-Rola trademark to Coca-Cola—to me a minor matter, whereas it seemed more than weighty to the CEO. I yielded gracefully.

My bagatelle, however, was considered to be of such an order of magnitude that the entire board of directors would have to pass on it. They could have done so in my absence, but perhaps they were curious to see me. I appeared at the appointed hour to face the entire fifteen-men and two-women board. I do not feel at liberty to describe the sumptuous setting of Coca-Cola's inner sanctum, nor the behavior of the board. I am now permanently bound to the Coke board—meaning that both discretion and delicacy require that I keep most of these details confidential. Two events, however, need to be mentioned.

I don't think that I'm being indiscreet for divulging that my words, "This is my counsel, Pandora S. Blight," caused a visible and audible stir. My Pandora is not only a handsome woman, but also a person with a marvelous sense of decor—one of many reasons why I married her. For professional occasions, she wears severely cut suits (usually gray or black), white silk blouses, but no cravat or similar androgenic accoutrement commonly seen around the necks of female lawyers or bankers. She has great legs and wears shoes with heels that are just a centimeter or two higher than those found on the feet of her professional female peers. But this time, she decided to be daringly different. She came clad in tightly cut, dark gray pants made out of Thai silk, which ended around the ankle in jodhpur-fashion, thus giving them just the faintest touch of Pakistani women's trousers. The jacket was made of the same material and again cut in a manner that subtly suggested a riding costume. I doubt whether a woman in pants had ever sat in the orange leather chairs, but pants seemed to be just the right costume for the typically male discussions that suddenly ensued. One of the directors, an investment banker, kept pressing me. "But what can you possibly do with twenty-five million dollars per year, *after taxes* that is. Even one tenth that sum—*net after taxes* and for life—ought to be more than ample." He looked down the long board table as if he expected vigorous assent, for the logic of his remark, and for attempting to save the corporation a few million dollars. Of course he was right, if he thought I had intended to spend all that on myself. I wouldn't even know how to do it, but it simply wasn't any of his business. I was about to make an intemperate remark, when Pandora interrupted. "Before my client answers this, would you excuse us for a moment?"

I wondered why she was making a fuss, when both of us had concluded that Coca-Cola had no choice but to meet my price. But I had underestimated Pandora's perspicacity. The banker's reference to one-tenth being sufficient had triggered her thoughts. We had concluded, she reminded me, that even one million per year (before *or* after taxes) would spoil us terribly, and that the rest should go to philanthropy. But which one? I favored spreading it around. "You can do an awful lot of good in this world with twenty-four million dollars a year." (At home, I didn't hesitate to say "dollars.") "True," she had conceded, "but think how much more good you can do if you focus on only one or two projects. Even twenty-four million can get diluted quickly when you spread it around. Furthermore," she wagged her finger the way my grandfather did, as if this were taught in law school, "just think how many people and organizations will be after us when word spreads that we have that much money to give away. In no time at all, lots of people will positively dislike us. Let's pick one place to start with." This made sense, and in a remarkably short period we agreed where the twenty-four million dollars would go.

I say "remarkably" because before Pandora met me, she suffered, like many people in this modern world, from chemophobia. She worried about the ozone layer, the global greenhouse effect, toxic pollutants, plastics, pesticides—and blamed all of it on the chemists. It took a long time and a great deal of my patience to convince Pandora (at least I *think* I convinced her) that the chemistry was okay; in most of the cases that worried her, the science was brilliant and so was its potential, provided it was used properly. The problems that concerned her also concern me, and I firmly believe that, eventually, chemistry will also provide most of the solutions. The real issue is how people use scientific or technological advances, especially when so many of the decisions about societal applications are made by scientific illiterates. The world might well be better off if we had more chemists and fewer lawyers in our government and legislatures. But the fundamental problem behind all the complicated environmental and ecological issues is not the number of chemists and lawyers but the number of *people* in the world—the extra billion we add each decade. What all that eco-spouting has to do with Coke is this: just a few weeks before my Roca-Rola patent application was allowed, the newspapers and TV were full with the news that after many years of supporting Planned Parenthood, one of the largest foundations in the country had yielded to the pressure of a vociferous anti-choice lobby—self-anointed the "Pro-Life" Movement—to terminate its annual contribution. Pandora was livid that this widely respected charity was prepared to ignore the biggest problem in the world because it was afraid of what the barking of a vocal minority might do to its donor base. But as the twenty-four million dollar Coca-Cola kitty suddenly appeared on the horizon, we decided that twelve million of it should be turned into an anonymous, outright gift to Planned Parenthood. The other twelve million would be converted into a challenge grant that would match every dollar contributed to Planned Parenthood by any business enterprise—large or small—with three of our own.

But now, outside the boardroom, Pandora convinced me to change our plan in a way that would make the board feel less exploited by a young scientist.

"Sir," Pandora addressed the banker director as soon as we had returned, "your earlier comment leads my client to announce a change in his demand." The banker looked pleased, but when I glanced at the CEO, I could see concern on his face. Perhaps he was thinking of my "after tax" modification. "My client's proposition is quite simple, but also nonnegotiable. That is, if your board does not agree to our new proposal, then we must return to the original one: twenty-five million *after taxes*." We were sitting at the end of the long table and Pandora let her look sweep, searchlight-fashion, around it.

"Well?" the banker prompted. "We'll take one million a year net after taxes," she said and stopped. The banker leaned forward. "Did you say one?" "Yes, sir. One," she replied quietly. "Your earlier point was well taken. What person could possibly need twenty-five million tax-free every year for life? But . . ." Pandora's pause extinguished the incipient triumph in the banker's face. "The remaining twenty-four million will be given in the name of the Coca-Cola Company to an organization of my client's choice. A tax-exempt organization," she raised her lawyer's index finger for emphasis, "with the IRS's stamp of approval. This proposal saves you quite some change: around sixteen million a year, since most of my client's taxes no longer apply, not to speak of the tax deduction on your twenty-four million worth of corporate largess."

"A bagatelle," I added, it suddenly dawning on me that a new word had entered my regular vocabulary.

"Is that the entire proposal?" The question had come from the CEO, not the banker. "For all practical purposes, yes." "What does 'for all practical purposes' mean?" shot back the CEO. I practically burst with admiration at the way Pandora handled the board: like a star matador, flicking the red flag here and then there. "Minor boiler-plate stuff," she replied in legalese, "of no financial consequence to Coca-Cola. First, the choice of the grantee organization is entirely up to my client. You have no veto—in fact, no say whatsoever in that matter. Second, all such contributions will be made openly and formally in the name of the Coca-Cola Company. And third, my client retains the option of requiring that part or all of your contribution be structured in the form of matching challenge grants, which might induce other corporate donors to participate in such philanthropy to my client's chosen institution. That's it. No other caveats."

"Could you give us some examples of organizations you might have in mind?" The question was posed by the only lawyer on Coca-Cola's board. "No," Pandora answered in the manner of a judge ruling a lawyer's motion out of order. "That's not relevant at this time." "But what if it were illegal?" the man persisted. "Any grantee put forth by my client will carry a bona fide IRS ruling of tax exemption under Sections 170 and 2055 of the Internal Revenue Code and we won't pick any religious institution. As far as a guarantee is concerned, that's all you need." For a change, Pandora was starting to get irritated, but it didn't matter, because the CEO had started to tap his pen on the table. The taps were not loud, but everyone noticed them. "I move that we accept counsel's offer," he said brusquely. "I second that motion," said the banker. I expected the CEO to ask for any discussion, but he asked immediately for a vote. The ayes had it. "Son," he looked down the length of the table at me, "you've got a deal for life." I can't blame him for calling me "son," because I'll have to concede that the last few weeks have made me behave like a smug kid who has won the granddaddy of all science contests. Still, it grated.

We were heading for the dining room. With one arm around my shoulder and the other around Pandora's, the CEO said, "I don't remember Coca-Cola ever making a twenty-four million dollar gift to any single organization. That'll make quite a splash."

"You have a point, sir" she mused, an inscrutable smile on her face. "Do you have anybody in mind for the first year?" Even though he looked at me, it was Pandora who answered. "*I* do," she said, simultaneously disengaging herself from his arm.

I wondered whether he'd caught the emphasis on the first word, but I shouldn't have. You don't become the CEO of a corporation the size of Coca-Cola's without a ceaseless radar searching for nuances. "What about you, son? After all, it's your money." I don't like to be patronized—especially not after just having earned twenty-five million for life after taxes—and I was about to say so. But before I could even choose the proper bon mot consistent with boardroom badinage, it dawned on me that I'd be repeating the scene with this CEO and his successors for decades. What IRS approved entity would get the next twenty-four million and the next . . . and the next?

"I'll have to confer with counsel," I said, "but only after lunch."

"You have a point," he said good-naturedly. "Important decisions shouldn't be made on an empty stomach. Come on, son," he added, while steering me into the dining room with his heavy hand on my shoulder, "first things first."

The Dacriologist

Excuse me, please," Jasper Gunderson mumbled as he made his way through the crowd. "Excuse me." He'd never been to a vernissage—he hadn't known the word when Bruce Rosen had first mentioned it—and when he'd found out from the invitation that it was only an opening, he'd almost decided not to come. Contemporary art was not exactly Gunderson's forte. At the front desk he'd seen a price list of Rosen's oils and watercolors. Most were in the $9,000 to $17,000 range. My God, thought Gunderson, I didn't know Rosen was in that class. Pushing through the jammed gallery, without even a drink in his hand, he was looking for just one painting. *Pat in Tears* was number 14, NFS. It was, he noticed, the only one not for sale.

Number 14 was in the side gallery, where the crowd was smaller. Patricia's portrait was a large oil—so large that the couple with their backs against it blocked its view only partly. It was a light gray canvas with the faintest outline of a human figure. Gunderson saw, after a moment, that the woman in the painting was shedding tears, not crying. To him, the dacriologist, the distinction was obvious: "shedding tears" was an operational definition, "crying" an emotional state. He felt as if Patricia were about to tiptoe from the mysteriously gray canvas into the bright room to confirm his diagnosis. "As usual," she would've said, "you're right."

The woman blocking his view was first to turn around when she noticed Gunderson trying to navigate around them.

"God, Chuck. Take a look! And we were standing right in front of it." She smiled at Gunderson. "Aren't these gallery openings terrible? We don't even pay attention to what's here. I guess you do, though, don't you?"

"I don't usually come to such events." The confession made Gunderson sound like an outsider. He decided to make up for it by some subtle upstaging. "I only wanted to see this portrait. Isn't it remarkable how Rosen almost forces Patricia to come at you if you keep your eyes on her?"

"Patricia?" The man walked to the wall to read the label. "She sure is crying."

"How do you know?" Gunderson asked sharply.

"What do you mean, how do I know? I can see tears. All you've got to do is look long enough."

"Just because you see tears doesn't mean a person is crying."

"Wait a moment, Chuck," interjected the woman. "Crying implies unhappiness. What the man meant was that just because you see some tears doesn't mean the woman was unhappy. Isn't that so?"

"Exactly," replied Gunderson. "That's what I meant."

"By the way, I am Valerie Hemming and this is Chuck Philpott."

"My name is Gunderson," he said, shaking her proffered hand. He'd deliberately omitted his first name, he wasn't ready yet to "Chuck" her friend, or whatever Philpott was.

"What's your first name?"

"Jasper," he admitted.

"So if she isn't crying, why the tears?" Philpott asked.

Gunderson stared at the painting. Without taking his eyes off Patricia, he said, "She just responded to some outside stimulus."

Valerie broke a silence. "How do you know?"

"I can feel it."

An awkward quiet had fallen over them when a cheerful voice intervened. "So you did come, Jasper. I wasn't sure whether you'd make it—you don't usually leave your lab this early. Well, what do you think of your star subject?"

"It's mesmerizing, Bruce. Do you know these people? This is Valerie . . ." The usual blank descended over Gunderson, but Philpott saved him.

"I'm Chuck Philpott. You must be Bruce Rosen."

Hands were shaken all around.

"We were just wondering why this woman is in tears," Valerie said. "Did I put it the right way, Mr. Gunderson?"

The grin disarmed Gunderson. "Quite."

"Mr. Rosen," continued Valerie, "you tell us: what caused the woman's tears?"

Rosen looked amused. "Why ask me? You're talking to one of the world's authorities, and Patricia was one of Dr. Gunderson's favorite experimental subjects. Isn't that true, Jasper? But I've got to go into the main gallery. There are lots of people I still have to greet."

"Are you a physician?" Philpott had turned deferential.

"No," replied Gunderson. "I'm a dacriologist." He said it dead-pan, expecting the usual question.

For once, he was disappointed. Before Philpott even had a chance to ask, Valerie interrupted. "Are you a soft or a hard dacriologist?"

"What on earth are you people talking about?" asked Philpott.

A triumphant smile was on Valerie's face. "*Dakrios,* Greek for tear."

"Valerie! How do you know this?"

"I majored in classics before going to Wharton," she said without looking at Philpott. Her hand was on Gunderson's arm. "Well, what's your answer?"

Gunderson enjoyed the unexpected repartee. He'd taken Valerie for a gregarious yuppie. "What's the distinction?" he asked. Sexual innuendoes had never before been part of his professional introduction.

"Oh, you know, Jasper." He liked the bantering way in which she addressed him by his first name. "Are you interested in the psychological reasons for tears, or do you study their composition?"

"I guess I'm a hard dacriologist with soft undertones."

"In that case, let's have dinner together," said Valerie.

In the elevator, Gunderson turned to Valerie. "Do you always invite men you've just met to dinner? And shouldn't you have included Philpott? He didn't look very happy when we took off so suddenly."

Valerie just shrugged. "Chuck's a bore. Besides, I'm surrounded by MBA types all day long . . ."

"Aren't you one? You mentioned having gone to Wharton." Gunderson felt unexpectedly relaxed. And curious.

"I sure am." She grinned. "That's why I invited you: I want to know what makes a dacriologist tick."

"'Tick'? What an analytical word!"

"That's the problem with us MBAs—we pretend to be analytical, but we're just nosy. But how did you get into tears? I'm fascinated by them."

"'Fascinated' is not the sort of word I usually hear in reference to tears."

"Do you like Indian food?"

"I can take it or leave it," replied Gunderson.

"In that case, tonight you'll take it. At Bikash's. It's just the place for a dacriologist."

Jasper Gunderson had been single for several years. Bachelorhood suited him—a number of fleeting romances, two serious liaisons, but nothing lasting. A dacriologist meets many women, but—as with shrinks—mixing one's professional and romantic lives is unwise, even dangerous. Patricia Maxwell might have become an exception, but then she moved in with Bruce Rosen, and he became friends with both. Right now, he was in one of those in-between stages when his personal antennae were particularly sensitive to women.

As Valerie discussed the dinner choices with the Sikh waiter, Gunderson had his first opportunity to examine her at leisure. She needed little make-up and evidently knew it: smooth, sun-tanned skin; a lower lip periodically moistened by the tip of her tongue; gray eyes displaying perpetual amusement; and brown hair, with a bleached streak, cut so dashingly short on the sides and at the back as to border on punk. Altogether a daring arrangement for an MBA.

But what had appealed particularly to Gunderson was the woman's almost mannish self-assurance, which he had first noticed at the gallery. Then, she insisted that they use her convertible—a Saab—with the top down. No sooner had he closed the door when she announced, "I don't want to argue at the end of the meal about who'll pay. Tonight, you are my guest."

"We'll start with samosas and masala popadum," she said to the waiter. "Then let's have chicken pall and the prawn vindaloo . . . and bring us also some chapati." She scanned the menu. "We've got to have some vegetables. How about some small portions of spinach bhaji and aloo sag bhaji? And some rice: the zaffarani chawal." The Sikh nodded. "Jasper," she asked, "have you ever drunk lassi? Let's be completely Indian tonight."

"I've never even heard of it."

"Good," she said. "In that case we'll order one salty and one sweet. This way you can experiment. And you'd better bring us some ice water," she continued, addressing the waiter. The Sikh smiled and left.

Valerie leaned across the table. "Jasper, now tell me what you meant—about being a hard dacriologist with soft undertones. I like the description—I might borrow it sometime and replace 'dacriologist' with 'MBA.'"

"You really want the whole story? How I started as an analytical biochemist, developing methods for detecting bodily trace constituents?" He'd assumed a faintly mocking professorial style, but Valerie was having none of it.

"Just make it short and pithy. How did you get into tears?"

Gunderson stopped playing with the chutney dish. "I couldn't resist the challenge of examining tears once I'd heard—six years and a couple of hundred volunteers ago—that we know less about their composition than about that of any other physiological liquid. It took a long time just to establish the composition of basal tears—the ones we produce all the time, that never run down our cheeks. I used two techniques, capillary gas chromatography and mass spectrometry."

"Come on, Jasper, get to the point!"

Gunderson looked startled. "In addition to classics, did you also study chemistry?"

"Of course not. But you're telling me about your work as a hard dacriologist. What I want to know is the soft side: what's all this chemistry leading to?"

Keeping his hands occupied was one of Gunderson's idiosyncrasies at meal times. He started to draw lines in the condensation on the water glass. "By now, I can map virtually all organic compounds in a tear so that I get the equivalent of chemical fingerprints."

"You mean each person has unique tears?"

Gunderson turned the glass around to find some unused surface for his doodling. "On the contrary, tears are pretty similar, even though the fingerprints are fairly complex. Our methods are so refined that we can detect the smallest traces—parts per trillion—of organic compounds. One day we found a difference between tears from male and female subjects. Tears from men contained metabolites of the male sex hormone, testosterone, whereas in women—depending on the time of their menstrual cycles—we encountered varying amounts of estrogenic and progestational hormone derivatives."

His companion looked impressed, the way laymen do at times when scientists pontificate. "Jasper, don't tell me you can tell from a woman's tears whether she's pregnant."

"Not yet. We haven't looked at enough different tear samples from pregnant women. But your question gets close to my interest in 'soft' dacriology. I asked myself: if one can detect traces of sex hormones, what about other chemicals that are associated with mood changes? Hormones like adrenaline or steroids related to cortisone that are produced under stress; substances like serotonin and other psychogenic factors. I figured that if we could accomplish that, analysis of tears might offer some insight into their origin—at the very least, whether they are tears of happiness and laughter or of grief and pain."

"And can you do this?" asked Valerie.

"We're well on the way," replied Gunderson. "What we need are data on many more volunteers."

"How do you collect the tears? How do you know whether the tears are indeed produced when the person was joyful or depressed? How do you . . . ?"

Gunderson raised his hands. "Did you invite me for dinner or for a crash course in dacriology?"

"Both," she said. "But here comes the appetizer. I'll give you a break while we eat the samosas and you try the lassi."

Gunderson took his time chewing. It gave him a moment to decide whether he should tell Valerie about Patricia Maxwell. Why not? he thought. If it hadn't been for Patricia they wouldn't be dining in this restaurant.

"Let me start with Patricia Maxwell, whose portrait you saw in the gallery. She was one of the first subjects—when we were still establishing baseline values under controlled conditions in the laboratory. We were looking for individuals who had a facility for lacrimation, who could easily put themselves into a tearfully depressed or elevated mood, and who'd be prepared to jot down what had made them cry at that moment. Incidentally, we always collect tears from each eye, so as to have two samples for each episode."

"You know, Jasper," Valerie said, "making your patients 'tearfully depressed' doesn't sound like a great thing to do to them. Or don't you call them patients?"

"No, we don't. They're not sick. Anyway, this is where Patricia came in. In the mood lab, within minutes, she could put herself into a happy or unhappy state and the tears would come pouring out."

"Mood lab?"

"It's a small room with a couple of comfortable chairs, a VCR, a record player with earphones, and a good reading light. That's all. We use videotapes, music, or books to get people into different moods that produce tears. After they've collected them, we ask them to define their mood numerically, on a mood thermometer . . ."

"Mood thermometer? You must be kidding."

There were times when Gunderson hated to be questioned about his research methods—especially the "soft" ones. Every time he passed the mood lab and heard muffled sobbing or screams of laughter he shuddered. Can a biochemist call this research? It always took some effort to sound convincing when he asked his subjects to complete a "Profile of Mood States"—a self-rating scale with lots of adjectives from which the psychogenic reasons for lacrimation could be deduced. Or the "Beck Depression Inventory," which at least sounded more clinical. Still, they gave him words and he wanted numbers. So he came up with the thermometer.

"It's just an arbitrary scale, from zero to one hundred. You'd have to be deliriously happy to measure one hundred and hopelessly depressed to rate zero. The numerical ratings are based on special questionnaires that our subjects complete right after they've finished collecting tears."

Valerie was listening with her elbows on the table, chin in her hands. "Go on."

"Well—Patricia was phenomenal. She could switch from one mood into another within minutes. Her tear composition was unbelievably reproducible. Once we'd picked up the presence of certain psychogenic chemicals in tears, we moved out of the mood lab into the field. Here, look at this." Jasper fished out of his pocket a small cellophane envelope. "This is a type of surgical sponge that we give to our field volunteers. These are people—mostly women, I have to admit—who are willing to contribute tears whenever they happen to cry. All we ask of the women is not to wear any make-up near the eyes and to gently dab any excess tears with this absorbent wad, put it into the envelope, and label it. The only other thing we request is that they measure their mood as soon as feasible on our thermometer scale. What we are trying to do is to accumulate a library of different chemical fingerprints—we call them dacriographs—for tears produced under various circumstances."

Gunderson was vaguely aware that he'd been lecturing, but Valerie didn't seem to mind. He was about to ask whether she wanted to enter his dacriological entourage—as he called his volunteers, though not to their faces—when the waiter arrived with their food.

"What should I start with? About the only thing I can recognize is the spinach."

"Try the main dishes, and see which one you prefer," replied Valerie.

Gunderson dipped into the chicken pall.

"Better taste just a little bit," Valerie said, but the warning had come too late. Gunderson was about to make a complimentary remark when the first burning sensation registered on his tongue. His next breath simulated bellows that had caught smoldering embers at just the right moment. Gunderson's obvious reflex was to get the burning stuff out of his mouth, but in his panic he chose the wrong direction: he swallowed it. Valerie had covered her mouth with her hand in a gesture of sympathy and to restrain laughter as she watched his eyes bulge and fill with panic. Gunderson drained his glass of water in one swig, but it was like water hitting sauna stones: a puff of steam and momentary cooling, followed by a wave of moist, even more intense heat.

He searched for his handkerchief to wipe away the tears but stopped before he found it to gulp down his almost untouched glasses of lassi, tasting neither the sweetness nor the salt nor the yogurt, and feeling only a slight diminution of the fire in his mouth. At that moment the Sikh arrived. Majestically he poured ice water into the glass, and with a moistened napkin wiped Gunderson's brow.

"How could you order something like that?" he gasped after downing his fourth glass.

"I adore spicy food, but I eat the pall with plenty of chapati. See?" she said. "Like this. Jasper, I'm sorry I did this to you. But chalk it up to professional experience. What do you think your own dacriograph would look like if you analyzed the tears that you just shed?"

"I'm not sure. There's a rare pathological condition—it's called a gusto-lachrymal reflex—in which a person cries the moment food is tasted. But we haven't bothered to analyze the tears of normal people who eat food like this." In spite of his smoldering mouth he was grinning. "I won't touch any other dish until I first see you do it."

Valerie took a bit of the prawn vindaloo. "This is very tasty, but not so hot; it's nothing like the pall. Here, try it."

Sitting back, she asked, "Would you accept me as a volunteer?"

"Why do you ask?" he said, stalling for time.

"I cry frequently. I try not to let it happen in the office. They'd just consider it a sign of weakness, but there's nothing wrong with a good cry, is there? Tell me," she continued after a pause, "have you figured out yet why one gets such a sense of relief after crying?"

Gunderson's mouth was partly open to receive the first prawn, but now he stopped. Using his fork, for emphasis, he resumed his lecturing style. "There's a man in Minnesota who thinks that shedding tears may be the way whereby the body gets rid of stressful chemicals."

"Is that true of all crying?"

The fork was swinging in time to Gunderson's shaking head. Both of them noticed the moving prawn and laughed. "No, certainly not all tears. For instance, I rather doubt that Frey—that's the man in Minnesota—would claim that the tears you saw streaming down my face fell into that category. It was the four glasses, not my tears, that helped me recover from the chicken. No, Frey was only thinking of emotionally stimulated tears—what we call psychogenic weeping. His hypothesis is based primarily on the observation that a subject exposed to freshly sliced onions produces a much smaller volume of tears than when the same person cries because of some emotional stress. But all he'd have to do is come here . . ." He gestured at the chicken pall. "It's still too early to tell whether tears are nature's disposal system for emotional wastes," Gunderson rather liked the metaphor, "but maybe we'll be able to provide some evidence for Frey's hypothesis."

"So now you're collecting dacriographs to tell why people were crying," Valerie said, "rather than to determine what the function of tears is?"

"Precisely."

"Well, in that case I want a bunch of your sponges and some of your emotional check forms. I'd like to run my own test. I'd like to check your"—she paused for a moment—"dacriological prowess before I make a commitment as a volunteer."

In the weeks following their dinner, Valerie provided several carefully labeled envelopes—the dates as well as the hours of tear collection were marked clearly—but she withheld the mood thermometer ratings and the Profile of Mood State forms. This was, her note read, to test the validity of Gunderson's dacriographs. He accepted the challenge, partly out of professional pride and partly because such circumstances justified his maintaining a social relationship with Valerie. She could hardly be considered an ordinary subject if she was unprepared to follow the standard protocol.

The first five samples came out well. Gunderson correctly identified two samples as "happy"—Valerie had privately rated them 75 and 82 on the mood thermometer scale—and three as "depressed." He even provided an impressive example of subdivision: one of the dacriographs had shown several characteristic "rage" peaks, whereas the other two fell into the conventional "sad" category.

One day Valerie called after lunch to announce that she would stop at the Wet Eye Institute to deliver a new sample. The first time Jasper had mentioned the name of his laboratory, Valerie had laughed.

Mildly irritated, Gunderson had pointed out, "There is a Dry Eye Institute in Texas"—he had refrained from identifying Lubbock as its location to avoid appearing too pedantic—"that studies various pathological states associated with excess drying of the eye." He had added, in a moment of scientific one-upmanship, that even the use of oral contraceptives had been found to affect tear volume.

"I brought you a special sample, collected early this morning. I'll be interested in what you find." They were in his small office, adjacent to the laboratory. Gunderson offered to show her around his professional empire—he was anxious to impress her—but Valerie refused.

"Some other time," she said. "I've got to get back to the office and you've got to analyze my tears."

Valerie's next set of dacriographs did not appear in Gunderson's office until three days later. The day before, he had sensed a strange disappointment in Valerie's voice on the telephone when she discovered that her earlier sample had not yet been processed.

To expedite his daily examination of dacriographs—dozens of them—he'd made some templates of certain standard ones, which had all of the characteristic chemical peaks associated with "happy" or "unhappy" crying, including some of the subdivisions that he'd been able to establish. As a matter of policy, Gunderson never scanned labeled dacriographs—he didn't want to be prejudiced in his evaluation. Only after he'd compared one particular graph with all of his standard templates, and been struck by the presence of two peaks that he'd never observed before, did he discover that it had come from Valerie's left eye. Half an hour later, he encountered a second such anomalous sample with the same extra peaks—from Valerie's right eye. It was standard practice in his lab to mix the dacriographs of tears from the right and left eyes of one subject with all the other graphs.

This offered an independent check of the validity of his analytical procedure: to see whether he could pick out the two matching samples from a large pile.

"Valerie? Where did your last sample come from?" It was only the second time that he'd telephoned her at the office. There was no chit-chat. "There's something peculiar about the two dacriographs."

"Why blame me?" she asked kiddingly, but with a note of pride.

"Can you get me another such sample? We'd like to check it again to see whether we can identify these new peaks."

"So I have new peaks? Yes, I can bring you a new sample."

"How soon?"

Valerie hesitated. "I'm in a meeting now. Let's see. Maybe tonight. Late tonight. Actually the morning is preferable. Yes; tomorrow morning. I'll drop them off on my way to the office."

On the following morning, Valerie's new specimen did not end up on the bottom of the pile. Gunderson had left instructions at the front desk to have Valerie personally bring the samples to his office. But Valerie didn't appear. The receptionist brought an envelope containing the two samples and a note: *Jasper—Call me when you have analyzed these, but not at my office. Ciao, Val.*

Only once had Gunderson been told to his face that some of his volunteers actually resented his ability to identify their moods from their tears. Patricia Maxwell had explained to him how his tear experiments had initially intrigued her; how she'd enjoyed contributing to his original analytical studies. But when he started to define her moods in chemical terms, she'd felt a sense of intrusion, which Bruce Rosen shared. "Listen, Jasper, I can't come back to your lab," she'd said. "I don't want my mood defined chemically. Bruce never questions me about my tears, but you should see the portrait he's just painted of me.

My feelings are all there, but I don't feel violated." Now he wondered whether Valerie's unwillingness to appear personally with her latest tear samples was related to Patricia's earlier feelings.

This time Gunderson analyzed Valerie's samples himself. When he found the two new peaks to be even more intense, he spent the rest of the morning refining the data.

"Valerie, I know you didn't want me to call you at the office, but I've just analyzed your last two samples myself. I think I'm on the right track. May I ask you a couple of quick questions?"

"I guess so," she said, with an impatience that didn't seem quite genuine. "But make it quick, I'm in a meeting."

"Valerie . . ." Jasper hesitated. "Have you by any chance just gone on oral contraceptives?"

"What?" she broke out laughing.

"Did you just start on the Pill?"

"Why, Dr. Gunderson! What a question to ask at three in the afternoon in my office."

"Come on, Valerie. This is science, not banter. The peaks in your tears are unusual steroid metabolites that might have come from one of the new types of Pills. Your first five samples didn't show them."

"I'm sorry to disappoint you, doc." She lowered her voice. "I've been on the same Pill for five years. Nice try, Jasper."

"Oh." Gunderson's disappointment was palpable. "Just one more question. At what point in your menstrual cycle are you right now?"

After a pause, she replied, "The end of the first week." She added, "I'll call you tonight, but it will be late. I've got a business engagement this evening."

When the telephone rang, Gunderson was conducting the third movement of the "Death of a Maiden" quartet with one hand while slowly turning the pages of the latest issue of *Biochimica et Biophysica Acta* with the other.

"What music are you playing?"

"Schubert," he said. "Valerie, can you produce such tears at will?"

"Almost."

"Can you do it anytime?"

"Theoretically, yes."

"What does that mean?" persisted Gunderson.

"It means just what it says. In theory, I could cry like this at any time, but in practice I don't."

"Does another person's actions cause your tears?"

"No," she said after a pause, "not necessarily."

"OK, I give up. Tell me how these tears are produced."

"Produced?" she echoed. "What an analytical word. Since I learned about dacriology at dinner, I guess it's only fair that I resolve this mystery of science for you at another meal. I'll cook it at my place, but I can't do it until Saturday evening."

As was his custom when he entered an apartment or someone else's home for the first time, his eyes swept the walls. To him, walls were a form of tattoo. The nature and placement of the tattoo told you a great deal about the person. Bare walls, though not bare skin, turned him off. But that was not the problem in Valerie's home. Most of the living room walls were covered with bookshelves, with the books attracting him like pheromones. Even the virtual absence of paperbacks registered with him. While she was putting the finishing touches to their dinner, he scanned the spines. Some of the economics titles were almost as incomprehensible to him as the Greek ones. There were leather-bound volumes of Ovid, Virgil, and Catullus, and an entire shelf of French literature.

"Do you also know French, in addition to your Greek and Latin?" he asked as she came out of the kitchen with an open bottle of wine.

"*Mais oui, Monsieur Jasper*," she replied, accenting his name on the last syllable and rolling the *r* softly.

After dinner, they sat on the sofa, sipping port and listening to Berg's "Lyric Suite." The only light was that of the four candles on the dining room table. Valerie, shoeless, was leaning against one corner of the sofa in her simple white silk kimono and pants, a black belt tied around her waist, karate style. "Content?" she asked, raising her glass.

"Content," said Gunderson. "But not satisfied. What about those tears?"

Valerie slid toward him, took the glass out of his hand and kissed him. She was naked under her silk garment, and not in a mood for foreplay. Gunderson had barely realized what was transpiring when he found himself on his back, with Valerie thrusting on top of him. Her torso was arched backward, her hands firmly clasping Jasper's outspread legs, until she collapsed on him with her gasps loud, her tears wetting his neck.

"Jerry, you do understand why I want this experiment to be kept quiet, don't you? This is not the usual 'if' experiment. If it doesn't work we'll do this, and if it does, we'll do that. This," he pointed to the blackboard, "has *got* to work, and when it's done, it's finished." Castor gripped the side of his desk, "Jerry, this experiment will be in all the textbooks; it's the sort you encounter once in a lifetime. Look how lucky you are: it's taken me over thirty years, while you . . ."

Castor's voice trailed off as he gazed at his young collaborator with affection and a tinge of envy. Stafford was his all-time favorite student, his Prince of Wales, and to that extent deserved this chance. But what a chance it was! If only he had been offered such an opportunity at the age of twenty-six!

When Castor resumed, it was business as usual. "Jerry, you do know what's at stake here? Let's go to work."

In less than three months Stafford produced the expected results. Castor was triumphant. He stayed up all night writing the first draft of the brief communication to be published in *Nature*—the most widely read journal in his field. The paper's authors were I. Castor and J. P. Stafford. According to Castor, the order was purely alphabetical, but one of the laboratory cynics had wondered why there were never any Allens or Browns in the group. There had been an exchange fellow from Prague named Czerny, but that was the closest alphabetical proximity to Castor that had occurred.

"A Generalized Theory of Tumorigenesis" was promptly accepted for publication. When the *Nature* article appeared, even Castor was staggered by the number of reprint requests. As journal subscription costs soar, reprints of specific articles are God's gift to scientists from soft-currency countries. Castor's secretary, whose brother was an avid stamp collector, was suddenly busy removing stamps from all the reprint request cards from Argentina, Bulgaria, India, and dozen of other countries. But then the colleague he respected most—Kurt Krauss from Harvard—called to say that this paper could not possibly escape notice in Stockholm.

"I. C., if I were an envious man, I'd now be bright green. But you know I'm not." His chuckle sounded almost convincing. "If I couldn't think of this experiment, then I'm at least glad you did."

Castor could feel the warm blush spill over his face. It wasn't due to embarrassment; just sheer pleasure. Krauss's Harvard was a place that counted Nobel laureates almost by the dozen. However, at Castor's midwestern university, only one Nobel Prize had ever been won, and that was in the 1930s. Getting a Nobel five decades later would put I. C. in a class all by himself. You couldn't do that at Harvard or Berkeley!

At such moments, scientific etiquette demands modesty. But as often as not the demure look toward the floor, the disclaimer with the hands look faked when seen. The telephone is kinder.

Castor rose to the occasion. "Kurt, I knew it was a good idea"—*good? It was the greatest idea I've ever had!*—"but I was also lucky. I've told you before about Jeremiah Stafford. The guy has golden hands—you've never seen such lab technique. I don't know if anyone else could've pulled this off."

"We all have people like that," Krauss chuckled. "It just takes talent to find them. Still, sooner or later, someone will have to repeat your experiment. You might as well have us do it. This way, you'll know who's providing the *Good Housekeeping* seal."

Climbers of Himalayan peaks count their glory in minutes. Hardly has the photograph been taken—flag in one hand, ice ax in the other—than the return to the last camp is already under way, lest the next storm approaches or the oxygen supply gives out. Not so with scientific Everests. For three months, Castor basked on the summit—at lectures, seminars, and symposia—where he presented *our* experiment. Was it a royal we or a true plural? One never knows with a scientist, who is taught in graduate school never to use the first person singular, even in the absence of any coworkers.

One afternoon, Kurt Krauss telephoned to say that one of his best associates ("You remember him, I. C., don't you? He's my Stafford.") had been unable to replicate Stafford's experiment. Such a failure was not unheard of in their field. After all, Castor and Stafford had only published a preliminary paper, without presenting all experimental details. Castor asked Stafford to prepare a precise description of the laboratory protocols so that they could be sent promptly to Harvard. Stafford agreed.

Within a couple of days, Stafford, who had never missed a day in four years of graduate school, called the professor's secretary rather than Castor.

"Stephanie, please tell I. C. that I caught the flu. I feel so lousy. I don't even want to explain to him why I can't prepare the report for Krauss just now."

The message annoyed Castor. Stafford, who had taken immediately to the eighty-hour work weeks in Castor's laboratory; who pronounced the word "vacation" with a disdain born out of scientific machismo; whom Castor had always found in the laboratory—why did he have to pick *this* time to get sick? Castor's annoyance escalated to real irritation when, a few days later, he was told that Stafford had telephoned from Florida: his grandfather had suffered a heart attack. "Where the hell is the man's loyalty?" he thought. "To his grandfather or to the lab project?"

Such gracelessness was not typical of Castor, but he was under some pressure because one did not keep Krauss waiting This Harvard professor was in a class by himself, and especially so when the validity of a key experiment was in question. Castor decided on a sloppy, but simple, shortcut: he would photocopy the appropriate pages from Stafford's laboratory notebook and send these to Harvard with a brief explanatory letter.

There was nothing improper in copying Stafford's laboratory notebook. In contrast to personal diaries, a scientist's diary is expected to be produced for inspection by others, on demand. Invariably such notebooks are solidly bound with pre-numbered pages, and all entries are written down chronologically. Like all great expedition leaders, Castor was fanatical about details. Everything had to be entered in the lab notebooks with indelible ink, not pencil; even trivial calculations had to be put into the notebook rather than jotted down elsewhere on loose sheets. Every graduate student starting out got the same speech: "You can't put too much into your notebook, but you can write too little. You never know which details may turn out to be crucial." When the students departed from Castor's laboratory, the notebooks stayed behind.

What Castor saw in Stafford's notebook bothered him. The experimental protocol was indeed there, but the precise details seemed surprisingly scant. After some effort, he succeeded in telephoning Stafford in Florida.

"I hope your grandfather is getting better," Castor left no opening for a reply, because he did not consider it a question. He continued, "Jerry, you know that Krauss is having one of his postdocs repeat *your* experiment. You know they're having trouble repeating it and I can't let Krauss wait much longer for the experimental details. I thought I'd simply send him copies of your lab notebook."

All Castor heard in reply was a low "Yes?"

"I hadn't looked at your notebook for months . . ." Castor could not continue, because Stafford had moved promptly onto the offensive.

"Well, you had no reason to do so. Except for our last *Nature* article"—there was no ambiguity about "our" in this instance—"you'd asked me to write the first draft of all of our joint manuscripts."

"Yes, I know." Whatever accusatory nuance had existed in Castor's earlier tone had now been muted. Unlike many colleagues he could mention, who hardly ever wrote drafts of manuscripts that bore their names as coauthors, Castor, until recently, had always written the first version. On more than one occasion, he had pointed with pride to the difference between his practice and that of the professorial nonauthors who nevertheless appeared as authors. Castor was unforgiving in his condemnation of such conduct. But even he, I. Castor—the superstar who had resisted the temptation of huge research groups in order to have time for scrupulous experimental confirmation and writing—even he had made an exception in recent years with Jeremiah Stafford. This exceptional treatment was only one of several subtle indications that Stafford was being groomed as Castor's successor. Except for Stafford, nobody in the laboratory ever called Castor "I. C." to his face. "Professor Castor" or, on occasion, "Prof" was established etiquette. Only outsiders or professional equals "eye-seed" Castor. Nobody remembered when Stafford had joined this select club. It was not that he had been specifically invited; one day he was just there.

Castor was now apologetic. "Jerry, I can't send just photocopies of your notebook pages to Krauss. There are too many missing details. Why, Jerry, you don't even indicate which buffer you used in the original extraction; you don't give the column support for your high-pressure liquid chromatography experiment; you don't say where the arginase came from . . ."

Stafford's' interruption was peremptory. "I know, I. C., but these are trivia. This is routine stuff, and you know what time pressure I was working under. Finishing what I did"—the first personal singular was verbally underlined—"in less than three months took some doing. I guess I was just sloppy with my notebook entries. Why don't you let me write up the missing details? I'll be back by Wednesday and you'll have them in your office first thing Friday morning."

This was what Castor wanted to hear. The letter to Krauss was mailed the following week.

In less than one month, Krauss called to say that his associate, an experienced enzymologist, had still been unable to replicate the key experiment. Castor gave the expected reply: "Kurt, I'll have Stafford repeat the experiment in my lab in my presence."

Krauss agreed that this was the most reasonable course; he assured I. C. that until he heard from him, the Harvard group would not publish their failure to repeat what had become known as the "Castor–Stafford Experiment." Naming an experiment or theory after the original authors is the ultimate historical accolade in science. However, it is rarely bestowed without independent verification, which Krauss had intended to provide.

Castor immediately summoned Stafford and presented him with the facts; the experiment could not be repeated in Krauss's laboratory. He suspected that a minor but essential experimental variable, not recognized by them, was the reason for their failure. He asked Stafford to perform the experiment with him in his private laboratory. The young man's temporary move into the professor's own laboratory caused considerable comment and even gloating among some members of the research group. After all, Krauss's initial failure to repeat the work outlined in their *Nature* article had not been kept a secret. While none of the students and research fellows had ever been asked to work in Castor's own laboratory, it was hardly a promotion that the professor's fair-haired boy had now been ordered to repeat his spectacular experiment under the watchful eyes of the master.

The weeks passed quickly and without difficulty. Of course, this did not mean much, because everything depended on the final enzyme assay, which was due on the following Monday. When Castor arrived in the morning, nervous and concerned, he met an impressively confident and self-assured Stafford. Within a few hours, Castor was in a joyous mood. The assay had come out as expected; the experiment had indeed worked. The professor announced the results at a special group seminar and publicly congratulated his favorite collaborator. He also used the occasion to do a bit of preaching about the importance of laboratory notebook discipline.

When Castor returned to his office, he found a sealed envelope that simply read "Professor Castor—CONFIDENTIAL." The message, typed and unsigned, consisted of only one sentence: *Why was Dr. Stafford in your private laboratory on Sunday evening?*

It hardly mattered whether unfounded suspicion, bred by professional jealousy, or something more serious had prompted that note. For Castor, the dilemma was enormous. The proper steps would have been to call in Stafford, to confront him with the accusation, to repeat the experiment without Stafford, and if he failed in the experiment, to inform Krauss of what had transpired. In addition, he would then have to undergo the expected public penance: a letter published in *Nature*, in which he would withdraw the "Castor–Stafford Experiment." The standard ending would be "pending experimental verification," but everybody would know that fraud was probably involved if Stafford's name was not included in such a letter. If Castor had put on this hair shirt, his tumorigenesis theory would have been just that: one more theory in the cancer field, cast upon an ever-mounting heap of discarded ones. Yet he felt in his bones that his theory had to be right. Even before this disaster, Castor had thought of a second experiment that might provide independent verification. It was risky, but Castor felt that there was now too much at stake—not the least of which was a possible Nobel Prize.

Castor decided to say nothing—neither to Stafford nor to Krauss. By saying nothing, he considered himself still unbesmirched by any possible scandal. Furthermore, instead of wasting precious weeks on another attempted repetition of Stafford's experiment—by thinking of it as "Stafford's," Castor had already passed mental judgment on the affair—he started on the new experiment, the one he had not mentioned to a soul.

Castor's sudden unavailability stunned his collaborators, but none more so than Stafford. In the past, most students, and certainly Stafford, were privy to what the professor was doing with his own hands. This time, even Stafford's request to see Castor in his laboratory was met by a totally unexpected response from the secretary, who usually just waved Stafford in: "I'm sorry, Jerry, but Professor Castor is working on a very important experiment. All I can do is take a message."

Stafford became frantic. He had always had open access to the professor's laboratory; now he was staring at a locked door. This exclusion of Castor's favorite set the lab's rumor mill going full blast. Stafford's anxiety became almost unbearable; he thought of writing a letter, but he wasn't sure what to say in it. Demand an explanation? Give an explanation?

In the end, no letter, nothing, was required. The second experiment—Castor's independent proof of his tumorigenesis theory—did work. He had vindicated his earlier optimism about the viability of his brain-child.

Rather than rushing into print in *Nature*, Castor played it cool and cautious. He telephoned Krauss: it was now unnecessary for the Harvard group to examine further the verification of the

"Castor–Stafford Experiment," because he had just completed a second and experimentally simpler one. In a subtle way, Castor forced Krauss to center his attention on his own experiment, and away from Stafford's.

"Kurt, just wait till you see the details. It's a beauty, but I won't write it up until someone in your lab has repeated my work. Before I publish this experiment, I want to be absolutely sure that nobody has problems repeating it. I'll send you copies of my own lab notebook by Federal Express. You'll get them tomorrow."

Krauss could not help but agree to become the irreproachable witness to Castor's scientific veracity. What nobody could predict at this time was that Krauss would also spoil Castor's triumph: when the great Krauss eventually published his confirmation of Castor's second experiment—of course, he waited until Castor's triumphant paper had appeared in *Nature*—he referred to that experiment, quite innocently, as the "Castor Confirmation." For Krauss and every reader, Castor's solo experiment simply confirmed the generalized tumorigenesis theory, whose authors were Castor *and* Stafford.

All this was still in the future. Since Castor was certain that his latest work would be confirmed at Harvard, he had no reason to delay announcing his success through the time-tested laboratory grapevine. He called a special departmental seminar and announced that he would be speaking—without listing a title. Only superstars can use such a ploy. Lesser lights run the risk of an empty room when the notice reads "Topic to be Announced."

In Castor's case, even without the mystery of an untitled talk, his virtual disappearance from public view for weeks would have guaranteed a jammed lecture hall. Stafford deliberately arrived late. As he sat in the back, he was convinced that he was about to witness his own public crucifixion. Shortly after Castor's start, it became obvious that

Stafford was not even a participant in the drama about to be presented to the hushed audience. Without referring to Krauss's inability to validate Stafford's work, Castor reported his *second* experimental proof of the generalized tumorigenesis theory. Within hours, the news had spread by e-mail to all key laboratories.

In the excitement, nobody had noticed that Stafford had slipped out of the seminar room just as the applause started.

He headed straight for the professor's office. "Stephanie." His voice was composed as he sank into a chair in the secretary's office. He acted as if the last few weeks had not existed. "I. C. just gave the most fabulous talk you could imagine. I just thought I'd wait for him here—I want to tell him what I thought of the seminar." Stafford did not mind that he had to wait for a long time; he knew that Castor would be surrounded by a throng of admiring students and colleagues at the conclusion of his lecture. It would give him time to rehearse his little speech.

Stafford was still silently debating whether to offer detached congratulations or bubbling enthusiasm when Castor appeared. The young man jumped up. "Prof"—he did not consider "I. C." appropriate under the circumstances and "Professor Castor" was clearly too formal—"could I see you for a moment in your office?" Castor merely looked at his student and then motioned him into the room.

As soon as the door was closed, Stafford switched gears. "I. C.—I just wanted to see you alone for a moment, because I knew that down in the lecture room you'd be surrounded by everyone. I just wanted to tell you that this was the most fantastic lecture I ever heard. I'd been concerned when I didn't see you for all these weeks, but now I'm relieved."

The older man's expression did not change. "You damn well ought to be," was all he said.

Climbing Everest by two different routes is sensational. Hardly anybody has been photographed twice on the summit. This time, Castor's basking there was terminated much quicker than the first time around. Again the message was from Harvard, the bearer Kurt Krauss: he congratulated Castor on the brilliant conception of the second experiment and informed him that the verification of Castor's results had already started. Castor felt elated; a potentially devastating situation was well on the way to a permanent resolution.

But then Krauss continued. "By the way, I. C., your man Stafford called. He asked whether I'd offer him a post-doctorate fellowship in my lab. He said that he'd spent all of his experimental life in your department, and wanted to work on some other problems before looking for an assistant professorship.

"With other people, I wouldn't even have called. But since he's working with you, I wanted to check whether you'd mind if he joined my group. I know your fabulous opinion of Stafford. But you're familiar with our red tape. We need some letters of recommendation in the files, and obviously, one must come from you. Actually, Stafford didn't even list you as a referee; he mentioned that he didn't want to bother you with such a trivial request. In reality I think he was worried that you might be annoyed that he wants to work in another lab."

Underneath, Krauss had felt somewhat guilty, which explained this avalanche of words. Now he waited for a response, but none came. For once, Castor was speechless.

Krauss mistook the silence for disapproval. He hastened on. "I. C.—you've got to admit that almost anything the man would do now in your place would be an anticlimax after the spectacular work the two of you published in *Nature.* Could you send me a letter about him? It needn't be long—just write what you've always told me: that he was the best man you've ever had in your lab."

A monstrous dilemma was now facing Castor. If he refused to send such a letter, he would have to explain the reason to Krauss. After all, I. C. could not just claim that he wanted to keep Stafford around, and therefore would not recommend his best student. But if he did write such a letter, Castor would never again be able to erase the "Castor–Stafford Experiment" without implicating himself. An enthusiastic letter of recommendation to Krauss would permanently close the door to such a withdrawal. In a flash, Castor realized that Stafford had challenged him with a piece of fiendishly clever blackmail. He decided to pay the ransom, and by May of that year, Stafford had departed for Harvard.

For thirty-five minutes, October 17 could have been called the shortest, best day of Castor's life. I. C. was an early riser, who needed no alarm clock. Shortly after six a.m., while he was showering, the phone rang. Castor had intended to let it ring, but the persistence of the caller finally drove him, dripping wet, to the bedside phone.

"Professor Isidore Castor?" The man's accented voice was unfamiliar; furthermore, nobody had called Castor "Isidore" for decades.

He decided to be noncommittal. "Who's calling?"

"Sven Lundholm from *Svenska Dagbladet* in Stockholm."

"Yes?" Castor was barely able to utter this single word, so full of suspense, desire, triumph, and some deviousness. He wanted to pretend cool detachment, but his heart was pounding. Every winner had wondered—gratefully, to be sure—why the first call invariably came from a reporter. "Yes," he added more forcefully, "this is Professor Isidore Castor speaking." *(Isidore Castor? My God, this sounds like a stranger!)* "What can I do for you?"

"I have the honor to congratulate you on your winning the Nobel Prize in Physiology or Medicine." Castor did not mind the pompous words; in fact, they had hardly registered. "I wonder whether you have any comments."

"Comments? No, I don't. I don't even know whether it's true." Castor remembered the embarrassment of Vincent Du Vigneaud, who publicly acknowledged his pleasure when a reporter congratulated him prematurely for winning a Nobel Prize. In Du Vigneaud's case, the reporter had been premature by one full year!

"Professor Castor!" The man sounded outraged. "Surely you do not believe that I am calling from Stockholm to make a joke?"

"How do I know you're calling from Stockholm?" Castor figured he could afford caution, even at the risk of insulting the caller.

"Do you want to call me back in Stockholm?" shot back the reporter. "I can give you the number of *Svenska Dagbladet*."

"Never mind," replied Castor, who was enjoying himself. "I'll comment, but for the time being it's off the record."

"How do you feel having won the Nobel Prize?"

Castor could almost see the reporter rise, as he pronounced the last two words, and bow from the waist. "Frankly, I haven't thought about it, but if it's true, it's a great surprise. If it's true," he repeated the words for emphasis, "then it's not just an enormous honor, but also recognition for the efforts of my entire team of collaborators over the years."

This was the sort of stilted answer that most reporters, especially Swedish ones, recognize as fake. The man continued on another tack. "Professor, what will you do with the prize money? Have you decided how to spend it?"

Castor was taken aback. "No, of course not. I haven't even thought about it." This time, the answer was totally correct but the reporter persisted.

"But you do know how much money goes with the prize?"

Again Castor replied honestly. "Well, I know it's a lot, but I don't know precisely how much."

It was a lot of money, but only half of what Castor had imagined. As soon as the Stockholm reporter hung up, Castor turned on the radio to listen to the news. He missed the key words by just a second or two. ". . . this almost completes an American sweep of this year's Nobel Prizes. Only the one in literature is still to be announced next week."

"Damn it," thought Castor. "Do I have to wait for the seven o'clock news to hear the name, or should I call the radio station?" Actually, he did not have to do anything. The first telephone call followed shortly thereafter. Kurt Krauss was on the line.

"I. C." His voice was warm and excited. Genuine pleasure flowed over the telephone. "I hope I'm one of the first to congratulate you. You really deserved it. I'll bet you'll be amused by what I have to tell you. Guess what the announcer said when the Nobel Prize in Medicine was announced this morning over the local Boston station?'

"I haven't got the foggiest idea," countered Castor.

"Come on," coaxed Krauss. "Just guess!"

"OK." Castor played along with his friend. "Midwestern cancer whiz wins Nobel."

"Wrong!" Krauss was triumphant. "He started out with 'another Nobel Prize won by Harvard man.' Can you beat our local chauvinism? It's typical of Harvard."

"I don't get it." Castor sounded puzzled. "Why should he have said this?"

"What do you mean, you don't get it? You Midwestern yokel! We are so damn anxious to add to our list of Nobel laureates, everybody here is including Stafford on the Harvard roster. Ridiculous, isn't it?"

"Stafford? You mean . . . ?"

The seeds for the Castor–Stafford combination were probably sown in 1923, when MacLeod and Banting won the Nobel Prize in Physiology or Medicine for Banting and Best's discovery of insulin. The outcry about the injustice of Professor MacLeod, the director of the laboratory, sharing the Nobel Prize, while young Charles Best, who had performed the crucial experiment, had been ignored, persisted for decades. Since then, the Swedes had almost leaned over backward to recognize a younger collaborator. In 1983, Milstein and Jerne, together with a much younger Georges Koehler, were only the most recent example of such a shared Nobel Prize; the Castor–Stafford combination probably seemed just to most. After all, the key paper—the one that succinctly, but unequivocally, described the generalized theory of tumorigenesis, together with its first experimental proof—had carried the names of both Castor and Stafford.

One of the common courtesies among new Nobel laureates is to congratulate a co-winner, before acknowledging the dozens or even hundreds of congratulatory messages. Yet Castor could not make himself write the conventional letter to Stafford, and strangely, the young man did not contact his mentor.

Like most serious contenders for the Nobel Prize, Castor knew all about the ceremonies: the actual award is presented by the King of Sweden on the afternoon of December 10, followed by a spectacular dinner and dance at Stockholm's lovely Town Hall. Later in the week, a major public lecture—subsequently published in book and journal form—is given by each winner. This lecture, more than anything else, represents the historical record of the winner's scientific immortality.

The weeks before the actual award of the Nobel Prize are clearly the best. Parties, interviews, accolades of every sort are the usual fare; the novelty has not yet worn off, the prize money has not yet been spent. Castor had no idea what Stafford was doing, but for I. C. the pressure was building up inexorably. All he could think of was the actual ceremony, when he and Stafford would stand together before the King of Sweden, with the world press covering every detail. But this was nothing compared to Castor's fear of the scientific lecture expected of him and of Stafford. Since both were sharing the Prize for the same discovery, common sense and courtesy would require that they consult each other to decide who would say what, and in which order. But Stafford made no move.

Late one evening in mid-November, after having received a letter from Stockholm asking him to present the first scientific lecture, to be followed by Stafford's, Castor could take the pressure no longer. He sat down at his desk to start on the text of his lecture. Pen in hand, he stared at the empty page for seemingly endless minutes, writing the words that subsequently caused such a sensation: "It is with heavy heart that I . . ."

Was this to be the preamble to a Nobel Prize lecture or to a suicide note? As he set these words on paper, Isidore Castor realized in a flash that it wouldn't make any difference. For once, there was no dilemma to be resolved.

Sleight of Mind

One trick always left me baffled. He prompted you to select a card, made you shuffle the deck after you'd replaced the card, and then asked you—gently, an apologetic smile hidden in the typically Japanese manner by his hand over his mouth—to spread the cards, faces down, all over the table surface. "Now separate them into two piles," he would say, with a motion of his hand over the scattered cards as if he were cutting a cake in half. After a moment's hesitation, he'd discard one of the piles and ask you to repeat the process until only two cards remained on the table. He'd point to one of them and without a further word, just a discreet gesture, dared you to turn it face up. Invariably, it was the card that you'd selected originally.

Professor Koji Nishinaka was an internationally known biochemist accustomed to showing off in front of huge audiences. He was a consummate performer—as a scientific lecturer as well as an amateur magician. "Amateur" was hardly the correct term: he didn't charge for his performances, but they were supremely skilled. His magician's repertoire covered everything from simple sleight-of-hand tricks—coins out of ears, vanishing handkerchiefs, all but the proverbial live rabbit—to phenomenal manipulations with cards.

This occasion, however, was no ordinary lecture. The audience was small: seven persons, all men, who had gathered for coffee and dessert after listening to Nishinaka give the annual Bowman lecture. Nishinaka was just warming up. He shuffled the deck with a speed and clatter that would have done honor to a blackjack dealer in Las Vegas.

"Quick! Pick one and don't intellectualize. Now put it back," he said, without taking his eyes off our host. Nishinaka quickly arranged the cards in a giant fan.

"Keep thinking of the card you picked," he reminded our host as he fingered one card after another. Suddenly he stopped, a card between his thumb and index finger.

"It was a spade, wasn't it?" To me, it seemed more of a judgment, but our host took it as a question. He nodded.

"Then it's this one," said Nishinaka, flipping the two of spades onto the table. He accepted the exclamation "That's it!" with a modest shrug: "All you need is practice."

The reaction of the group was typical of academics, and especially of men who claim to be professional seekers of answers. Several explanations were bandied about—all of them in the third person, as if Nishinaka had become invisible.

"I bet he saw the card reflected in Gilbert's pupil. Didn't you see how he was staring at him?"

"Maybe the cards are marked in some way—after all, they're his cards."

"It could've been a fingerprint. Did you notice how he examined each card after shuffling?"

I was grinning like an impresario—after all, I'd nominated Nishinaka for this year's Bowman lecture—when I realized that one man had remained silent: our Nobel laureate, the neurobiologist. He'd come to the Bowman because he chaired the selection committee for this prestigious affair, which includes a medal and a handsome honorarium. Furthermore, Nishinaka's topic, "Sensory Perception and Communication among Invertebrates," interested him. But the reason that he'd stopped after dinner was out of pure and nasty curiosity. At the Bowman committee meeting, apropos of nothing, I'd brought up Nishinaka's phenomenal card tricks. Nishinaka would have winced if he'd heard me use the word "tricks"—he considered the term demeaning—but then he wasn't present when I bragged about it.

"I suggest we invite Professor Nishinaka in spite of such non-scientific credentials," our Nobelist had interjected, "and then have a post-prandial examination by this committee of extrasensory perception among higher vertebrates." He'd winked at me, but instead of winking back, I'd looked down. Suddenly, I'd gotten worried.

Our Nobelist was usually *primus inter pares* and this time he played the role to the hilt.

"Professor Nishinaka, that was quite clever," he said with his dangerous lupine smile that I'd seen at many a scientific lecture. The speaker expected a compliment; instead it was a preamble to a question, innocent in tone but devastating in content. Looking at us rather than Nishinaka—as if he meant to say "watch me take care of him"—he asked, "Do you need to touch the cards?"

"I don't."

"Do you have to be present when the card is selected?" he continued.

Nishinaka hesitated. He was accustomed to questions after his performances, but usually they were not cross-examinations. "No, not really," he replied, after a pause.

"You don't? Then what *do* you need to do?"

The answer came instantaneously. "*You* need to do something first. You've got to be willing to concentrate on the card while I look you in the eye. To think of the card rather than trying to figure out how I do it."

There was a faint smile on the Nobelist's face as he turned to our host. "Gilbert, do you have any cards in the house?"

Nishinaka flushed before our host could even respond. The implication behind the request was obvious, but he let it pass.

"Yes," said our host. "We may even have a new deck. I'll be back in a moment."

The cards were still in their plastic wrapping. "Thanks," said the Nobel laureate as he aimed the torn wrapper into the wastepaper basket. "And now, Professor Nishinaka, would you be good enough to excuse yourself?"

As soon as Nishinaka had left, the Nobel laureate rose and went into a corner of the living room. In plain sight of all of us, he carefully separated the deck by holding the cards at their edges with the tip of his fingers—the way someone might handle a stack of hot plates. It was clear that he intended to leave no fingerprints, nor was he letting any of us see which card he'd chosen. His shuffling was slow and clumsy. But there was no derision, no sound. We all understood that we were observing a scientist eliminate one more experimental variable: a moist fingerprint on the clear surface of the brand new card.

The Nobel laureate returned to his seat and placed the stacked cards on the table immediately in front of him. "Would one of you please call the man?"

As I left the room, the laureate's voice—the contrast between his earlier "Professor Nishinaka" and the contemptuous "man" he'd just used—grated on me. I wanted to make it up to my fried. "Koji," I remarked, patting his shoulder, "they're ready for you. Good luck."

"Thanks," was all he said, his demeanor an untroubled mask.

"Professor Nishinaka," announced the Nobel laureate before I'd even closed the door, "I'm the only one who has seen the card in this stack here on the table." He motioned with his head toward the tightly packed deck. "Which one did I pick?"

The question was asked with such uncharacteristic bluntness that I sensed an undercurrent of concern; as if he wanted to say, "You aren't really going to try, are you? You can't possibly guess which card I chose, can you?"

I've always been impressed by the way some Japanese can assume uncomfortable positions and maintain them for what seem to me intolerable periods of time. Nishinaka, who was exceptionally tall for a Japanese, quickly squatted on his heels in order to face the Nobelist at eye level. He was so close that his adversary unconsciously drew back in his seat. There was a nervous silence as the rest of us grouped around the two men. They reminded me of Sumo wrestlers ready to spring. Nishinaka said nothing. He had fastened on the Nobelist's eyes like a magnet on an iron bar.

After a disconcertingly long silence Nishinaka slowly shook his head. "It's not a numbered card," he murmured as if he were talking to himself. "No, it isn't. Am I right?" he asked somewhat louder, addressing his challenger.

"That's right," was the curt reply.

The head shaking became more pronounced, the low monologue even more hesitating. "I can't catch it. It's not the queen, it's not the king . . . it's not a jack . . . not the ace . . . it's a black card. . . ."

The Nobelist's eyes had hardened, his lips were pressed together tightly. He said nothing.

I'd always assumed that there was some gimmick behind Nishinaka's card tricks and that one day he'd be exposed. But this time I was totally on his side—I felt like his promoter, his trainer in the ring, before a slightly hostile audience. I wanted my man to win. Come on, I prompted him silently, it must be the joker. For God's sake, man, speak up!

I found Nishinaka's concentration almost too painful to behold. His forehead was so wet, I wanted to offer him my handkerchief. "I don't understand it," he mumbled. "It's not a number card, no figure . . . it's not the joker. . . ."

Not the joker? I thought. What the hell is left?

"I've never seen such a card," he mumbled. "It's black . . . there's writing on it . . . but I can't read it." Suddenly he rose towering over all of us who were sitting around the low coffee table. He sounded angry, not defeated. "Show me the card," he commanded brusquely.

I looked at the Nobel Prize winner. His face was flushed as he reached for the stack of cards and slowly searched through them. Finally he found the card. He stared at it momentarily, then threw it on the table—face up—and abruptly left the room.

All of the men, except Nishinaka, bent forward to look at the card. When I saw it, I was amazed. "Koji, you were right. It's not really a playing card; it's just a promotion for this brand of cards. Evidently, they stick them into new decks before they're wrapped."

Nishinaka just glanced at me. It was neither triumph nor pleasure that I saw in his face. "No wonder I couldn't read him," he blurted out, "the man's envy always got in the way."

Maskenfreiheit

I'm a very fast reader, a skimmer really. I never wade through the documents before the board meeting begins; I go over them quickly while Rodney Hohmann, the company's chief financial officer, is still clearing his throat and shuffling his papers. I'm ready with my "outsider's" questions, which the inside directors, who are also part of management, must take seriously, like it or not. I would never want my fellow directors to know how little preparation I do, but this morning I realized that I would have to pay the penalty of strict attention because I had left the board book at home.

Unfortunately, Rod is a classic droner. After a brief but losing struggle with my attention deficit, I let my thoughts go to the preceding night's dinner with Sylvia, who was home from Berkeley. Sylvia liked German, she had said, because nouns could easily be combined to produce new ones that, though not found in any dictionary, were "perfectly kosher." Such ad hoc combinations were a concise way of describing complicated concepts for which one would need at least a sentence in English. "Take *Maskenfreiheit*," she announced with a touch of aggressive amusement. "Heine wanted to describe the freedom acquired by wearing a mask, so he simply strung together the German words for 'mask' and 'freedom.' Here's another one: *Lebensweisheit-spielerei*: life's-wisdom-playfulness."

"What about it?"

"It," she said, "was used by Wallace Stevens!"

"Ah," I offered, remembering a fragment from English 3B, "The Emperor of Ice Cream."

"Dad, everybody knows 'The Emperor of Ice Cream'! But not *Lebensweisheitspielerei*—you should look it up."

I'm rather proud of my daughter; but after dessert, I tried to regain my dignity. I asked as innocently as I could, "Doesn't *Maskenfreiheit* lead to *Lebensweisheitspielerei*?"

"What did you say?" Sylvia sounded downright suspicious.

Afraid I was mispronouncing, I decided to deliver the punch line myself. "The wise playfulness associated with wearing a mask leads to freedom in life, doesn't it?"

"Papa!" she exclaimed—she called me Papa very rarely—and threw her arms around me. "*Ausgezeichnet!* Papa, you're just like me. When I'm curious about something, I want to follow it all the way. Did you know I got interested in the history of masquerades? I started with Byron's letters from Venice. Papa, you've got to read some of that stuff." And then she informed me that the Venetians not only wore masks to hide their identities; it was clearly understood by everyone that in such disguise, boundaries of accepted behavior could be crossed with impunity. "Do you know, Papa," Sylvia said, pushing her chair closer to mine, "if somebody in Venice didn't have his mask with him, he could wear a small lapel insignia to indicate that he wanted to be *considered* as wearing a mask. When his friends saw that sign, they actually pretended not to recognize him!"

As Rod Hohmann plodded along, this struck me. Behind my director's mask, my non-director *persona* was off limits. For the first time in two years on the board, I studied the other men. Six white shirts (counting my own), two blue ones, and one tan sport shirt (Robert Claxton's). Five with deep red ties, the company logo discreetly woven into the fabric—a Christmas gift to all the directors—three striped Countess Mara ties, and one ascot. I realized that I'd never seen Bob Claxton with a tie. Turtlenecks in the winter, open shirts with ascots—or on occasion no neckwear—the rest of the year. Six pairs of glasses, five horn-rimmed or set in silver or gold, one (Claxton's) rimless and connected to his ears with very thin flexible straps—cat gut or strong silk thread, I guess—which were practically invisible, almost like a pince-nez.

That practically nobody wore a ring surprised me. Except for the chairman, who wore a small signet ring on his pinkie, and me with my wedding ring, all the directors were ringless. I'd assumed that most were married, but why was I so sure? Our conversations had never turned to families. All I really knew of the rest was what I'd read in the annual proxy statements: age, education, stock ownership, principal occupation, other board memberships. They were strangers, middle-aged or older, although they addressed me—and I them—by first names, as if we were buddies from way back.

Claxton was clearly the odd man out. And his behavior was even odder. The rest of the men were focusing, or pretending with varying degrees of success to focus on Hohmann's presentation. A couple were doodling and one was having trouble swallowing yawns, but this was acceptable director's behavior. Claxton was continually writing in a stenographer's notebook, every once in a while looking up at Hohmann, as if catching some particular phrase. He sat across from me, on the other curve of the oval, left elbow on the table and cheek in hand, so as to shield completely the notebook from his neighbor on the left. Everybody else was looking toward the speaker at the head of the table; I was the only one watching Claxton. Each time he looked up, I closed my eyes. At board meetings you're always given the benefit of the doubt: closed eyelids are meant to imply deep concentration.

I realized that I had not the foggiest idea what Hohmann had been talking about. I hadn't paid attention, nor had I skimmed ahead through the board book. I decided to borrow Claxton's, so I slipped him a note. He hardly looked up from his scribbling as he pushed the book across the table. As I turned the pages, looking for the financial report, I came on two loose sheets. The first sentence sprang right off the page:

"Well, Nicholas, what's your definition of friendship?"

I stopped to glance at Bob. His head was bent over the page on which he was writing, rapidly. I tilted the board book up at an angle so that neither Claxton nor Dan Lazare on my right could see what I was reading.

What's my definition, Nicholas Kahnweiler's definition, of a friend? Does the word have gender? Are there differences between ovarian and testicular friends? Of course there are. What, then, is my definition of a male friend? I've thought of one, but I won't tell him that yet, it might put him off. It's simple: a friend is a person in whose presence you can cry, who isn't embarrassed by your tears. Even shedding a few tears is significant, but crying, real crying, counts. Have I ever cried in a man's presence? I don't remember. Oh, I've had tears welling up in my eyes—especially in the theater—but when did I cry?

I never cried in front of Manya—only to myself, after she left. I'd cried about the misery of our marriage, what it could've been but never became. But that doesn't count, that's precisely the point I'm trying to make about friends. Crying to yourself is a physiological response, or a manifestation of self-pity. An adult crying in front of another adult is—no, not "is" but "can be"—a form of unveiling in which men rarely engage. If, just if, someone should touch you while you cry, a hand on your shoulder is enough.

The man broke into Kahnweiler's introspection. "Nick, if you can't think of a definition, what about a person whom you can trust without reservation?"

I'd better stop talking to myself. "Tell me," I said, "do you confide in many friends?"

It was a strange combination of embarrassment and curiosity that kept me from looking at Claxton. Hohmann had finished and the group had turned to something much more exciting: a possible corporate acquisition. Even Claxton had stopped writing. I closed the board book and slid it across to him with a gesture and a smile. He nodded.

The discussion became lively, but I couldn't focus on the topic. There was Claxton, asking questions as if he'd never thought about anything else. How could he switch gears so quickly? What was the connection between the two pages I'd just read and what he'd been writing until a few minutes ago?

The chairman announced the usual coffee-toilet-smoking break. I realized that here was an opportunity for some *Maskenfreiheit* research.

"Bob," I asked, "are you staying overnight in the city?"

"Yes," he replied. "Why do you ask?" It was the closest thing to a personal conversation that we'd had since he joined the board.

"Well, I thought if you didn't have a commitment tonight, I'd ask you to join Hilary and me for dinner at home."

"At home?" There was an awkward silence. Finally he said, "Thanks, that's very nice of you." I wondered whether curiosity or loneliness had made him accept. Or was he being polite?

Claxton rang the bell at exactly seven o'clock, as if he'd been standing behind the door checking his watch. By the time I reached the front door, Hilary and Bob were already exchanging introductions. In her hand she held a wrapped bottle of wine that he had brought.

"Shall we open this for dinner?" she asked.

"As you wish." He sounded both formal and impatient as if he wanted to dispense with all social preambles. While Hilary was still in the kitchen, Claxton wandered around the living room like a commissar in charge of cultural evaluations. The pictures on the walls elicited no comment, but he pulled a book from the shelves. "Did you like *Herzog*?"

"*Herzog*?"

He handed over the book.

"I'm afraid I haven't read it."

"Have you read any Bellow?" he continued.

"No."

"But you have several of his books." He pointed to a shelf. "Why do you bother having them here?"

"Hilary and Sylvia, my daughter, are the fiction readers in the family," I replied.

"What *do* you read?" Claxton stressed the second word in what seemed a mocking way. I was about to object when Hilary announced dinner.

As we started on the salad, Hilary spoke up. "Mr. Claxton, my husband hasn't told me anything about you except that you're on the same board."

"You see, Bob," I interrupted, "we've hardly touched base since I came home."

"How long have the two of you known each other?" my wife continued.

"Over a year, haven't we, Bob? As I recall, you joined the board last December."

"I think your wife wants a more precise answer, Oliver." There was something artful about his smile as he addressed Hilary. "Oliver and I have known each other for a total of about sixteen hours. Isn't that right, Oliver? Our board meetings don't really last longer than four hours."

It was the sort of answer Hilary appreciated: precise, but touched with a flavor of flippancy.

"Tell me, Oliver," Hilary began. She usually calls me "Ollie." "Oliver" put me on edge. "How much do you really learn about each other at such board meetings? My husband belongs to lots of boards," she'd turned again to Claxton, "but he usually doesn't talk about what transpires."

"Good for you!" The exclamation was addressed to me. Claxton's warmth surprised me.

"Do you get to know each other at all in sixteen hours spread over a year?" Hilary persisted.

"No, we're Venetians. We wear masks at our board." I thought I was being clever, but I realized that Sylvia's attentions to Papa last night had caused me to forget that Mama had also been present at her lecture.

"Are these masks a director's fringe benefit?" asked Hilary.

Claxton seemed to be getting more animated. "That's a very good point. I'm sure most of us wear masks at such meetings. I certainly do."

"Haven't you wondered what's behind some of these masks?" The challenge was thrown at both of us.

Again Claxton answered first. "On occasion, yes."

"What about today's meeting?"

"No, not today."

I don't know what made me say, "Bob was busy writing."

He gave me a brief, searching look. "So you noticed?"

"I couldn't help noticing," I said. "You sat across from me and you were writing most of the time."

"Did you wonder what I was writing?"

"Sure I did." I tried to be offhand. "You were writing all the time in that peculiar notebook."

"Peculiar?"

"Well," I replied, "it was a stenographer's notebook and there were yellow pads in front of all of us. I figured you couldn't possibly be making continuous notes on Hohmann's presentation. It was just too dull."

Claxton tugged on the strings of his glasses. "Oliver, does the name Kahnweiler mean anything to you?"

I blush rarely, but now I felt myself coloring. "Hmm, let me think," I offered, rising from my chair. "Hilary, I'll clear the salad plates and bring the casserole. You keep our guest amused."

The interval was sufficient to erase my blush—the effect, I reflected, of having your mask yanked off your face in front of witnesses. It gave me time to come up with a plausible response to the Kahnweiler question.

"You asked about Kahnweiler, Bob," I said in a voice that insinuated that this was a simple, everyday type of question. "Wasn't he Picasso's first dealer? I always forget his first name. Was it Daniel-Henry or Henry-Daniel?"

"Daniel-Henry," interposed Hilary. But then she went on, "Ollie is a collector of esoterica. Doesn't he show it at your board meetings?"

"Well," Bob's smile seemed rather forced, "he does ask a lot of detailed questions, but they always seem to deal with business. Nothing esoteric as far as I can recall. But tell me about Oliver, the collector."

"Oliver doesn't collect *things*," said Hilary, referring to me as if I were absent, "but *information*. There are times when I think he has a giant pin-cushion into which he sticks all those obscure items. I have a feeling these pinheads contain microchips that can store a lot of information. At the right time, Oliver just picks up a pin and inserts it into his personal computer." She tapped me on the head, a little condescendingly, I felt.

"Now it's your turn, Mr. Claxton," continued Hilary. "What were you writing this morning?"

"Tell me," he asked Hilary, as if he hadn't heard her question, "do you have many friends?"

"Yes, I suppose so," she replied cautiously. "But what makes you ask?"

"Intimate ones?"

"Yes. Some are intimate friends." Hilary was getting annoyed.

"Both women and men?"

I looked at Hilary, who had started to color. "Mostly women."

"What about Oliver?"

"Oliver? He's my husband!"

"I know that," said Claxton. "But husbands or wives are not necessarily intimate friends."

"Tell me, Mr. Claxton, are you married?" Good old Hilary was going on the offensive.

"No," he replied quietly. "I'm divorced."

"I see," said Hilary as if she were addressing a witness in front of a jury and had just made her point. "Any children?"

"Two."

"How old?"

"Are they boys or girls?" I interjected. I had no idea what Hilary was driving at, but at least I could pretend that I did.

"Girls. Eighteen and twenty-one."

"Are they your friends?" Hilary was calming down.

"Yes, I would say so."

"Intimate ones?"

"I guess this depends on one's definition of intimacy," he countered.

"So what is your definition of intimacy, Mr. Claxton?"

"That's a good question, isn't it, Oliver?" Bob hadn't changed the tone of his voice.

"Well, it's a pretty complicated one," I said. But Hilary came to the rescue.

"Come on, you two. Don't complicate a simple issue: an intimate friend is a person in whom you can confide; whom you can always ask for help without feeling uncomfortable."

Again Claxton pulled on the strings of his glasses. I'd never seen him do this at board meetings. "I had another definition of intimate friendship—primarily between males—but I have no quarrel with yours. One last question. May I?"

"Go ahead."

"Using your definition, is Oliver an intimate friend? Do you confide in him?"

"Of course." Hilary's answer came instantaneously.

"Really? You always confide in him?"

Slowly Hilary turned toward me, her full gaze focusing on my eyes. "No, not always," she said without looking away.

I was flabbergasted by the direction this dinner conversation had taken. Why, I wondered, had I been foolhardy enough to invite a virtual stranger to what was rapidly turning into a *masque à trois*? But I was in no mood to be questioned myself. I headed for the kitchen. Slowly I took the coffee beans out of the freezer and filled the coffee grinder. I put the burner on medium so that the water would take a few more minutes to come to the boil, and moved to the kitchen doorway. For the moment I preferred the role of listener.

"Actually, what do you do when you're not a director?"

"I'm working on a novel, my first."

"You, a corporate director? Why?"

"I guess I wanted to analyze myself publicly, behind the mask of a *roman-à-clef*, but now I'm enamored by metaphors and style. For a change, I want to write something where style counts—not the usual technical business verbiage. I've been looking at some books by real craftsmen. I guess I'm trying to prime my pump."

"Before you get too wet, watch out for clichés." Hilary was passably good at repartee.

"Good advice. But here's the kind of thing I'm now picking up. I just reread Saul Bellow's *Herzog*. I know you've read it."

"How do you know that?"

"Oliver told me so before dinner."

"Ollie? Why in heaven should he have told you that?"

"Just ask your intimate friend. I read *Herzog* slower and slower, until it took me several minutes to complete one page. I stopped at each sentence; I asked myself, how did the man think of this phrase? At one point Bellow is talking about an old bathtub—a trivial enough object that hasn't much to do with the story—and describes its enamel edge as 'wreathed with hairlike twistings, like cooked rhubarb.' I decided I'd see how I would have said this, but I just got stuck in the vegetable patch: 'cooked celery' is all I came up with."

"Celery hair isn't as thin as rhubarb hair," interrupted Hilary.

Claxton broke into laugher. "You see, you're getting caught in the same net. Of course you're right. Then I thought of cooked salsify."

"What's that?"

"That's the trouble with salsify. It's too clever. Rhubarb is common; everyone knows what it is, but few would've used it as a metaphor to describe hairlike twistings."

As I put the coffee pot, cups, saucers, and an open bottle of port with three glasses on the tray, I could still hear Claxton's animated voice in the living room. Through the open kitchen door I saw the two of them sitting next to each other on the sofa. Something made me stop at the doorway again.

"Take one of my favorite poets, Wallace Stevens. Occasionally I make up combinations of individual words that Stevens used in his singular way. What do you think of *aspic aplomb*?" Claxton waited. I could see Hilary's right hand playing with her hair.

"You mean 'there was aspic aplomb in her eyes'?" she asked.

"Not bad. But it wasn't that."

"So what did Stevens write?"

"First tell me your association—quickly—with the word 'aspic.'"

"Tongue."

"Tongue?"

"Tongue quivering in aspic. Haven't you eaten cold tongue in aspic?"

"What word would you guess Stevens combined with aspic?"

"Tell me." Hilary was going for the bait.

"Nipples."

"Nipples? Aspic nipples? You mean nipples that quiver?"

Claxton laughed again. "Hilary, I take a bow. But Stevens would've been shocked. I think it's our post-Freudian sexual fantasizing: aspic quivers, breasts quiver, when you eat aspic you almost suck it in, sucking nipples . . ."

"Stop it, Bob." Hilary giggled. "What did he mean?"

"Bitter nipples. Exactly the opposite. The line goes something like, 'how is it that your aspic nipples for once vent honey.'"

"I love the ambiguity of 'aspic.'"

Why doesn't Hilary leave the topic? I thought. And how had "Mr. Claxton" turned so quickly into "Bob"?

"How about 'the quivering aspic of her pupils'?" she continued. "Come on Bob, just look at my aspic eyes."

"I am, Hilary," he said.

The tray in my hands tilted slightly, rattling the cups. Claxton's voice stopped in mid-sentence.

Hilary turned around casually. "What took you so long, Ollie?" Addressing Claxton, she added, "You should see how quickly he makes coffee in the morning."

My God, I thought, she does have aplomb. As I put the tray on the coffee table, I asked, "What were you two talking about while I was slaving away in the kitchen?"

"Bob was just telling me about your meeting this morning." I had never realized how smooth Hilary could be.

I tried to be nonchalant, unsuccessfully. "What specifically?"

"Oh, just chit-chat." Of course, nobody confides totally *all* of the time, I thought. Still . . .

"Let me bring some cookies," she said brightly, and escaped into the kitchen.

"Cream and sugar?" I asked Claxton.

"No, thanks." And then he took me by surprise. "Oliver, your response earlier on about Kahnweiler was clever, but you do know why I asked you that question, don't you?"

"Yes," I replied. "Do you want some port?"

"Then why did you answer that way?"

"What did you want me to say in front of Hilary?" I countered.

"What's wrong with the truth?"

"How about some port?"

"Did you read all of it?" he persisted.

I nodded.

"Why?"

"Come on, Bob. What would you've done if you'd opened the board book and found those pages?"

"I would've closed it immediately and returned it to you."

I was about to tell him that I didn't believe it when Hilary reappeared. "Chocolate mints, anybody?" she asked, as she brought in a plate, the dark brown squares arranged in a spiral shape. Hilary pays attention to the appearance of such things. I took two but Claxton just turned his palm up, like a traffic policeman.

"You two look as if you'd been talking business."

"We were," I said.

"Too bad." It's amazing how at time two words can be full of ambiguous meaning.

Claxton looked at her. "It was related to masks—the kind that give you freedom. The question is, what right does a man have to look behind a mask without the bearer's permission?"

"What was your answer, Ollie?" she asked.

"We hadn't gotten to that yet," interjected Claxton. "If Oliver doesn't mind my doing it in front of you, for a change I'd like to take a look behind his mask."

"For a change?"

"Tell me, Oliver, what's your definition of friendship?"

It wasn't the question I had expected. "I hadn't thought of it," I said, "but I guess I agree with yours."

This seemed to mollify Claxton, who started to pour himself some port. But it didn't satisfy Hilary. How could it? "For heaven's sake," she exclaimed. "What are the two of you talking about?"

For a moment Claxton and I looked at each other, and allowed ourselves to smile.

Hilary didn't appreciate her abrupt and involuntary transformation into an outsider. "You know, your boards are like fraternities. I never hear you mention any women, Oliver."

The bubble of male conviviality was punctured. "I'm sorry, Hilary. Of course we'll tell you."

But Claxton stopped me. "Hilary, do you keep a journal?"

"Yes," she said. "I've kept one for years. Why do you ask?"

There was Hilary, to whom I've been married for twenty-six years, announcing to a virtual stranger something that I, her husband, never knew.

"I thought so. In that case," continued Claxton, "I'd like to ask both of you a question."

He pulled out his notebook, tore out two pages, handed one to each of us, and his pen to Hilary. "Oliver, do you happen to have a pen?" I reached into my jacket. "Would the two of you write down your answer—just a simple yes or no—to the following question. Suppose you walked into a room, here in your house, and inadvertently found an open notebook lying on the table. Suppose further, you took a look at one of the pages and realized instantly that it was the private diary of your spouse. Incidentally, Oliver, for argument's sake, I'm assuming that you're also the keeper of a journal. Are you in fact?"

"No, never."

He ignored me. "Knowing now that you're looking at your spouse's private diary, would you continue reading it? Remember, you're not being observed; you're alone in the room."

Before I could protest, Hilary had scribbled her answer, folded the paper, and handed it over to Claxton. Trapped, I did likewise.

Claxton shuffled the two sheets in a rather ostentatious manner and then unfolded them. "I thought so," he said. "Come Hilary, explain your answer to the fraternity jocks."

"What is there to explain? Of course I wouldn't have continued reading the diary. What do you take me for? It would've been an unforgivable intrusion into Oliver's privacy. I don't think I could live with somebody who'd do that."

"Don't get angry. I feel the same way. I just wanted to hear it from you out loud." That's all he said, with the two pieces of paper still in his hand.

"Aren't you going to ask Ollie?" But Claxton had now taken the two pages, lined them up, one on top of the other, and folded them in half. He ran them a couple of times between thumb and index finger to make a sharp crease and then extracted a fat Swiss army knife from his jacket pocket. He used the scissors to cut out a triangular wedge halfway along the fold and a second straight one, an eighth of an inch long, just below it. Carefully, he shaped the top of the folded sheet into a half moon. For a moment, he inspected his handiwork and then, using the end of the scissors, he poked a hole through the upper portion of the folded papers. Hilary seemed mesmerized by the performance.

Finally, he separated the two sheets and partly unfolded them. "There you are," he announced as he set them in front of our coffee cups. "A mask for each of you!"

It was true. It was almost spooky how these two pieces of paper, with our one-word answers on the back, had been transformed into two identical masks, the final stab with the scissors having produced the eyes.

I'd been thinking of how I'd explain my answer. I wanted to be candid and point out that my "yes" simply meant that satisfying one's curiosity was neither devious nor premeditated. Still, I was grateful that the matter seemed dropped.

"Hilary," Claxton said, "earlier on you seemed annoyed when we both laughed at you. I think we laughed for the same reason: embarrassment."

"Come on, Bob . . ." I began, but Hilary cut me off.

"Why were you embarrassed?"

"At dinner time I told you that I had a different definition of friendship from yours, primarily because I had been thinking of friendship between men. That's the theme of the novel I've been working on."

Now it became my turn to interrupt. "How come you're writing fiction at a board meeting?" There I was at the meeting, attempting to behave and certainly dressing like a proper director; and there was Claxton in his own private world, just because he was wearing a director's mask. Did he actually have the gall to think that he was earning his director's fee while diverting himself with his damn novel?

"But why not, Ollie?" cried out Hilary. "Didn't you tell us earlier how dull you'd found the man's presentation? What was his name?"

"Hohmann," Claxton said, enjoying himself.

"Listen, you two directors," remarked Hilary, "let's all forget about that board meeting. What I want to know is your definition of friendship. From both of you!"

Claxton looked at his watch. "It's getting late," he announced, "and I still want to do a bit of writing in my journal. Oliver can tell you all about friendship and you can tell him about director's masks. Or maybe the other way around."

After seeing Claxton off, I offered to take care of the dishes, but Hilary insisted that we return to the sofa. I shrugged and followed her into the living room. As I sat down, I noticed that she was staring at the miniature paper masks standing in front of our coffee cups. I was about to ask whether she wanted more coffee, but it was too late.

"Ollie, why on earth did he make these little masks?" she asked slowly as she started to turn over the one in front of her cup, the mask on which I had written my answer to Claxton's question. "They give me the creeps."

First-Class Nun

Michael Brewis always avoided eye contact on airplanes. It was his way of announcing that he wasn't interested in casual chit-chat. On this flight, as he walked down the aisle to find his seat, he was gratified to note that he had no neighbor. The distant gaze, the fixed look at the page, the pretense at dozing—none of these, it seemed, would be necessary. He had just placed his open briefcase on the empty seat beside him, however, when he heard a woman's low voice. "I believe that's my seat."

Brewis barely looked up as he gathered his papers and closed the briefcase. Without a further word, the woman slipped into her seat and opened a book before he'd even started on his papers. Soon after takeoff, the flight attendant came around offering a dinner menu, which he stuffed, unread, into the seat pocket. He always ordered a special meal ahead of time, usually a vegetarian dish or a fresh-fruit plate. On this occasion he had decided on fruit for the trip to New York and a vegetarian platter for the return to San Francisco. Even though he was concentrating on his paperwork, he waited for the second interruption, the attendant's question, "And have you chosen your dinner entrée?" But when the question came, it was addressed to his neighbor, not to him.

"Sister Olivia Fitzsimmons?"

"Yes?"

"Did you order the vegetarian meal?"

"Yes, I did, thank you."

"Would you like anything to drink before dinner?"

"What white wines do you have?"

"California Riesling and white Zinfandel."

"No Chardonnay?"

"I'm afraid not on this flight."

"In that case, just some soda water with lime."

Brewis looked sideways at his companion. Sister? British nurses are called sister, he thought, but the accent was east-coast USA with a slight southern nuance. A nun? He'd never before met a nun, or even seen one, in first class. How come she's so choosy about the wine? Is that what they drink in their cells?

His silent questions were interrupted by the flight attendant: "What can I bring you, sir?"

"I've also ordered a vegetarian dinner."

"Oh, there must be some mistake; we were given only one for this trip."

"But I ordered it weeks ago," protested Brewis. "I always order it when I make my reservations."

"I'm terribly sorry, sir. Somebody must've goofed."

"Perhaps I'm responsible for this mistake," interjected his neighbor. "I only ordered mine yesterday. Why don't you take it? I'll order something else."

"I wouldn't think of it," replied Brewis. He turned to the attendant. "I'll have the fish."

"What will you have to drink?" she asked.

"Nothing right now." He was aware that his refusal sounded petulant, but he hardly ever drank on plane trips.

As the attendant left, Brewis's neighbor remarked in a low voice: "You're irritated, aren't you? It's not really worth it—maybe the fish will surprise you."

Brewis, who was not accustomed to being evaluated, had turned toward the woman. For the first time he studied her carefully. He couldn't tell much about her body—she was dressed in a brown wrap-around skirt, her legs out of sight, a light-brown, high-buttoned, long-sleeved blouse covering most of her torso. She wore no jewelry except for a necklace with a silver cross, and absolutely no makeup. He focused on her face: light brown hair, pulled tight around her head into a bun; flawless complexion; full lips; and wide-open, intensely green eyes.

"You look as if you're about to ask me a question." A hint of a smile had crept into her eyes. "Go ahead. Why don't you?"

Again Brewis was taken aback. He, the professional questioner, was not used to being prompted. "You're right. When the woman addressed you as 'Sister,' I first thought of an English nurse, but as soon as you spoke . . ."

"You mean my accent?"

"Yes, and something in your tone. I concluded that you must be a nun, but . . . well . . . you don't look like one."

"You mean I don't wear a nun's habit and I'm not holding a prayer book?"

"I didn't look at your book."

"Well, look at it."

Brewis took one glance at the proffered book cover. "*The Church and the Second Sex*? I've heard about it. Are you interested in feminist ideology?"

"Very much. And how do you know that Mary Daly is a feminist?"

Brewis was pleased by the unexpected aggressiveness. "I'm interested in women," he replied, "in the role they're playing in contemporary society, and especially roles they should play." He realized how stilted this sounded. "Are you surprised?"

"Actually, yes."

"But then I have to admit that I'm surprised to find a nun reading such books."

"You don't know much about nuns, do you? Some of us live in the present." The green eyes sparkled as she continued, "Now that you've met your first one, you're burning to ask the next question, aren't you?"

"Yes." He enjoyed being egged on. "When did you become a nun? What made you do it?"

"In my twenties, after I finished graduate school, in philosophy."

The nun looked too playful, somehow too worldly, to be a philosopher, Brewis thought. "What made you decide to go from graduate school to a . . . ?"

"You're hesitating," observed the nun. "Is it because you're thinking of a nunnery but don't want to say it? You could always call it a convent."

Some philosopher, he thought, always on the offensive. "You seem to anticipate everything I'm about to say."

"Not really. It's just that we hear this all the time, especially from men."

Her bantering undertone caused him to be formal. "Sister, don't embarrass me. It's just that 'convent' has a medieval ring that doesn't fit you. You're dressed conservatively—but you're not in a nun's habit; you could be an everyday woman, and a very handsome one at that."

She laughed openly. "You really do have all the stereotypical responses. You mean a nun can't or shouldn't be attractive? Besides, you've really only seen my face."

Quickly he shifted gears. "But you travel first-class. You're choosy about what wine you drink—somehow I don't associate any of this with a convent, and most certainly not with a nunnery."

"You're right," replied the nun after a moment's hesitation, "about the first-class seat. Just to set the record straight: we always travel economy-class. This time United had oversold, and when I told them that I simply had to get to San Francisco tonight for an engagement that I couldn't break"—to his surprise, the nun blushed as she pronounced the word "engagement"—"they put me in this empty seat."

Brewis finally saw his opening. "Tell me," he asked, "why did the woman call you sister? How did she know you were a nun?"

"How did she know?" echoed the nun and looked out the window. After an awkward pause she rushed on. "When the agent at the gate told me that I should've checked in earlier, I explained that I had trouble getting a cab at the convent. The moment I mentioned the word 'convent,' he changed his tune. He handed me over to the flight attendant and told her to 'be sure to take extra care of Sister Olivia.'" She shrugged her shoulders. "You see, I was not pulling rank."

Brewis was not ready to let go. "What about the rest—your dress, the wine, the book you read?"

"That only shows how little you know about nuns."

"I know nothing about them. Actually, I know very little about religious life. You're talking to an agnostic from way back."

"Let me guess," retorted the nun. "You must be a scientist. Am I right?"

"No, but what makes you say that?"

"The almost aggressive tone in which you said 'agnostic from way back.' If you don't mind my asking, what's your occupation?"

"I'm a headhunter," he said matter-of-factly.

"You're what?"

It was not the first time he'd heard such a response when he used that term to describe his occupation. "I run an executive search agency. I interview people for top management jobs."

"Is this how you interview people—the way you're questioning me?"

For a moment Brewis gazed at the nun as if to determine whether there was more to her remark, and then his eyes wandered, past the woman, through the plane window to the wing flaps shuddering in the jet stream.

"No," he said slowly, "I'm not interviewing you. But I'd like to know something about a nun's life—I mean your present life. What brought you here?"

It was her turn to study him. "All right," she said finally. "It won't hurt an agnostic headhunter to learn something about nuns. You probably think only of the dictionary definition of a nun—a woman belonging to a religious order, living in a convent under vows of obedience, poverty, and chastity. Have you heard of the Order of the Carmelites?"

"Yes. But what's special about them?"

"I'll try to make it brief. The origin of our order is somewhat uncertain, but can probably be traced back to a twelfth-century retreat on Mount Carmel. Incidentally, the Carmelite houses are called monasteries, not convents. Because of our hermit origin and emphasis on solitude, no more than twenty-one nuns live in any one monastery, each occupying her own cell. Nobody else enters such a cell, only the prioress, and she must be invited. This is very different from other orders, say the Benedictine, in which several hundred nuns may live in one convent and sleep in dormitories." Suddenly, she stopped. "I must sound like a tourist guide. Tell me, are you really interested in such details?"

"Fascinated! But I'm wondering when you're going to get around to explaining what you're doing in that dress."

The nun nodded eagerly, as if her tourist guide license depended on her reply. "Most of the time we wear brown, but as you can see by looking at me, we Carmelites—at least in America—don't necessarily wear a nun's habit. Of course, we're not fashion plates. We buy sensible skirts, blouses, sandals—what I'm wearing now was ordered largely out of an L. L. Bean catalogue."

Brewis's amused expression produced another blush in her face. For some unexplained reason he felt pleased. "Please, go on."

"Our house in Brooklyn is one of the more modern ones in North America. There are others, not far from ours, that do not differ much from the Carmelite monasteries of several centuries ago."

"What do the nuns do in your monastery?"

"It depends on the house," replied Sister Olivia. "Some lead a very cloistered life, not unlike what the general public thinks nuns do. Others are very different. In our Brooklyn house there are nineteen nuns, and you'd be surprised how diverse their backgrounds and interests are. I am supposed to be a spiritual counselor . . ."

"You, a counselor?" The term unsettled Brewis. Only a few days ago, his wife Claire had announced that he should see a therapist. "Damned shrinks," he'd sputtered to her. "What are they going to tell me that I don't already know?"

"I am a counselor—largely for outsiders who wish guidance or advice." She hurried on, as if she were wishing to change the subject. "Among my fellow nuns are a photographer and a musician."

In spite of his alerted caution, Brewis couldn't refrain. "I suppose Poulenc is her favorite?"

"Why?" The nun seemed nonplussed.

"You know, the *Dialogue of the Carmelites*." Michael Brewis frequently indulged in what his wife used to call "cultural braggadocio."

Claire hadn't meant it as a compliment, but he couldn't drop the habit.

The woman looked at him anxiously, as if caught unprepared. "I'm afraid I don't understand."

Brewis might have persisted in showing off, but this time he resisted the temptation. "Oh, never mind. What other occupations do you have?"

She seemed relieved. "We have a couple of writers and run a small press. You were surprised about my reading. Of course, we live with the Bible and with religious books, but our concept of spiritual and religious literature is a broad one."

"Sister, your mention of books has triggered a question in my mind." He turned to face her more directly, as he always did when he searched for information. "Those vows you mentioned—I'm curious about them. For instance: how does obedience jibe with the feminist book you're reading?"

"I'd rather start first with poverty, in other words worldly possessions," countered the nun. "We really lead a rich life: rich in content and rich in privacy. If you're interested in intellectual or spiritual endeavors, modern life offers you little time or place for contemplation. That, and companionship with kindred spirits, with other women, are important, especially in this male-dominated world. So why should some nuns not be interested in feminist ideology? After all, the role of women in the Church is now a topic of hot debate, at least in some religious circles. Now do you see why I'm reading Mary Daly's books?"

He persisted. "Sure. But how do you handle poverty of possession? For instance, you were rather emphatic about wanting Chardonnay. Are you a wine connoisseur? And if you are, how did you, a nun, become one?"

"You sound a bit like a district attorney . . ."

"I didn't mean to," protested Brewis.

"I'm just joking," said the nun. "Of course you're justified in asking about the wine. I joined the Carmelites when I was twenty-six years old and my parents frequently had wine at dinner. Besides, my father-in-law was a wine importer—"

Brewis couldn't restrain himself. "Your father-in-law?"

"I was married before I joined the order." The brevity of her reply made clear that this was not a topic to be pursued.

"Occasionally, we have wine at dinner at the monastery, but cheap jug-wine. In a way I'm glad there's no Chardonnay on this flight—there is no reason to remind oneself of an earlier life that one has left voluntarily. . . ."

Her voiced trailed off as she sipped on the glass of soda-water. Suddenly, looking straight ahead, she began again, in such a low voice that Brewis strained to hear.

"In a way, I'm being tested all the time by temptations from my past. Not in the big ways you might imagine, but in little ones that most people don't even think about. It's particularly true at meal times. It's not just the wine, it's items like cheese or fish. For instance, we always eat processed cheese in the monastery. Many a time my mouth waters for a good strong Stilton or Camembert, but when my turn comes to do the shopping, I return with Velveeta, even though I could've saved money on some other purchases and bought a more interesting cheese. Or fish: in our house, it's almost always flounder. In fact, these days it's mostly frozen flounder, now that we have the microwave—a gift from the family of one of our nuns. You know, we get gift packages all the time. I myself put a stop to it with my family . . ."

"Why?"

"It was when my brother sent me some Godiva chocolates. You know, it's really trivial what I'm telling you. Temptations such as these are easily resisted—"

"Unless you're traveling," interrupted Brewis.

Sister Olivia looked at him as if she were searching for a hidden motive behind his comments before returning a fleeting smile. "Perhaps these temptations prove that it isn't so easy to forget one's former life or even to decide what is and isn't a temptation. Especially in a modern religious house where the nuns have frequent contacts with the outside world."

"Let's take a more subtle example." By now Brewis felt in complete command of the conversation. "What about intellectual connoisseurship, say in books?"

They were interrupted by the flight attendant, who had come to set their tables. "Would you like some wine with your meal?"

Brewis repressed a laugh and gestured to his neighbor.

The nun turned to him. "What would you recommend?"

That was elegantly done, he thought. "Oh I think if I were you I'd just order water."

Without hesitation, Sister Olivia turned to the waiting attendant. "I'll follow the gentleman's advice. Just water for me."

"And you, sir?"

"You said earlier that you had no Chardonnay, but I've forgotten what white wines you have on board."

"Riesling and white Zinfandel."

"From what vineyards?"

"Both from Almaden."

"In that case I'll just have water," replied Brewis.

As soon as the woman had left, Sister Olivia said, "This little performance was for my benefit, wasn't it?"

"I suppose so."

Her reply surprised him. "There's nothing wrong with acting, provided you stay in character."

"Did I?"

An impish smile crossed the nun's face. "Probably."

Michael Brewis, the experienced interviewer, decided it was time to change the subject. "Are you free to read anything you wish? You implied—no, you actually said—that in your monastery the definition of religious books is a very broad one. Surely there must be some limit to that broad definition? Take some fiction that is downright anti-religious. As a nun, are you permitted to read such books? I don't mean by your prioress. Do you permit yourself exposure to such books?"

Sister Olivia had been nibbling at the salad, but now she stopped. "There is no black-and-white answer to your question. In the more traditional Carmelite monasteries, the answer is simpler. But in our Brooklyn monastery, we have much more exposure to the outside, which, of course, also includes books and other literature. In addition, our professions frequently require that we familiarize ourselves with a great deal of secular literature. My own activity as a counselor is a case in point. To that extent, each nun must make individual judgments and sometimes that isn't easy. It's certainly more difficult than rejecting Chardonnay."

The changes in her conversational style puzzled Brewis. Now she sounded again like a guide reciting a standard line. "You said that each Carmelite nun has complete privacy in her cell. It seems to me that it would be very simple to smuggle any reading material into your cell."

"You make it sound like a girls' school, where the students are trying to circumvent the system. I've probably oversimplified the decision-making power of the individual, even in as modern a house as ours. There's a considerable amount of peer-control. If I want to purchase a book, I usually need to pay for it from our communal funds. I won't be told, 'Buy this book but not that one,' but most of my sisters will know what book I've bought. If one of the nuns—not just the prioress—thinks that it's an inappropriate book, she'll say so. We'll then discuss it, and if a debate arises other nuns will join in. Of course, I could 'smuggle' a book into my cell, as you put it, but personally I can't conceive of doing it. This doesn't alter the fundamental dilemma you've pointed out—the conflict between temptation caused by connoisseurship and our emphasis on poverty."

Brewis nodded pensively. "What about your other vow, obedience?"

Sister Olivia answered almost eagerly. "That's a simpler question. The outside world looks on obedience as a burden. Of course nuns are obedient to the prescriptions of their religious tenets. It's what brought them together. But primarily they're obedient to a standard of morality that's not difficult to accept if you compare it with the values of the outside world."

"And the vow of chastity?'

"What about it? Remember, women of all ages enter the order. Some are virgins, others have led an active sexual life." There was no hesitancy, no demure look at the floor: she kept her eyes straight on Brewis as she continued. "They know what they're doing. Abstinence from sex is not always so enormous a sacrifice for women as many people, notably men, think."

My God, thought Brewis, I can't believe it. Have she and Claire been talking to each other? He felt embarrassed, but he asked the question anyway. "Do you often talk about this subject?"

"I told you earlier that my primary function in our house is to provide counsel and that I do not just see nuns. There are no boundaries to what a counselor discusses."

"Do men also come to you for guidance?"

"Indeed. Why do you ask?"

Brewis didn't know how to introduce the subject of Claire: the wife who was about to walk out on him. In his professional life, he was essentially a headhunter for men, or at least male types; the few women he'd encountered mostly fell into the same category. In his private life, Brewis hardly remembered meeting a woman where sex didn't actually or potentially enter the equation. But this was totally different.

"You look pensive. Are you bothered by something I've said?"

"No, not at all," he said quickly, almost apologetically. "I was just thinking about your counseling work. I've never had any professional contact with shrinks. I'm sorry, I should've said 'therapists.' A verbal habit—probably some stupid reflex on the part of a supposedly strong man who thinks that he should be able to solve all of his problems by himself and that a therapist is a crutch. Or to put it another way, if you need to unburden yourself, do it with a friend."

"There are times when a friend is the last person. Do you open up often to a friend?"

"I guess not. Perhaps it's an occupational hazard. I spend most of my time analyzing others. I seem to have lost the ability or even inclination for self-analysis. Maybe it's my profession: I'm really a matchmaker, with the corporation as the bride for whom I'm interviewing suitable husbands."

Brewis looked straight ahead. This way he could pretend that he was speaking to himself. "As I listened to you, I was almost wondering what would happen if I, the agnostic headhunter, the impersonal matchmaker, were to talk to a spiritual counselor."

A sudden and remarkable change occurred in the nun's demeanor. It was as if she knew what would follow, and wanted to stop it before the question was actually raised. "Everybody can benefit from therapy and especially from spiritual counseling," she said. And then the curtain dropped. "I hope you won't think me rude, but I've suddenly gotten quite tired." With these words she reclined her seat and closed her eyes.

Brewis began to read, but he couldn't focus on the pages. He kept reflecting on what had transpired. How he'd been on the verge of making an extraordinary request to this nun: to be his shrink, to show him how to talk to his wife. According to Claire, every person has only a certain quota of understanding and he, the headhunter par excellence, was draining his cup of empathy daily at the office. And just when he, who usually questioned others without disclosing anything himself, was ready to relinquish his standard role, the nun entered her cell and closed the door. Brewis simply couldn't figure it out. Eventually, as the cabin darkened for the movie, he fell asleep.

The captain's voice woke him, announcing their impending landing in San Francisco. To his surprise he found that he'd slept for over two hours and that the seat next to his was empty. Brewis looked around to see whether she had moved elsewhere in the first class cabin. At that moment, Sister Olivia reappeared and slid into her seat. He quickly turned, ready with a polite remark, but the woman seemed oblivious to his existence. Her attention was completely focused on rummaging through her bag. When Olivia Fitzsimmons finally straightened up, she caught the full force of his stare. Her smile was vaguely apologetic as she pointed to the small bottle in her left hand. "I always have problems with my ears plugging up when we land." Tilting back her head, she placed a few drops of decongestant into each nostril. "I hope you had a good sleep," she said just as the plane's wheels touched the ground.

They were among the first passengers to deplane. Brewis decided that he would ask the nun for her address. Why not bring up point blank his request about counseling? he thought. They had reached the end of the narrow gangway and were about to enter the lounge when the first flash momentarily blinded his eyes. "Peter, you shouldn't have," exclaimed Sister Olivia to the man who had thrust a huge bouquet of yellow roses at her. Cradling the flowers in her right arm, she smiled smartly at the cameras with the flashbulbs popping one after another.

"Peter, darling," Brewis heard her coo. "Wait till you see the script. It's better than *Agnes of God.* You should've seen the convent. . . ."

Noblesse Oblige

Sybil Stirling was in no mood for an examination, but there was sure to be one. Arturo was her first live-in significant other, at least the first she'd mentioned to her parents. Should she have prepared Arturo? It had seemed better not to; he'd likely become defensive in an aggressive sort of way.

"*Mi amor*," she'd started. She'd never learned how to roll the *r*, but she knew he liked to be caressed in Spanish by this very WASP daughter of a very WASP family. "My parents are here for a banker's convention. I got tickets for the theater—"

"What to?" The interruption was typical of Arturo Flores. Even though he'd stopped working in the Public Defender's office, he still acted on occasion like a trial lawyer.

"*The House of Bernarda Alba*. I know you like Lorca. This is Tom Stoppard's version."

The young man's smile lingered. "Will your parents like it?"

Sybil shrugged. "We'll see. But I know they're looking forward to meeting you. What do you think about St. Honoré's for dinner? It used to be my father's favorite restaurant before they moved east. Stuffy, but first class food."

"And terribly overpriced," Arturo had added.

"Don't worry, my father always picks up the tab. But have you been to St. Honoré's?"

"Someone once tried to impress me by taking me there."

"And did he?" she asked coyly.

"No, she didn't," was all he said.

Sybil Stirling had an extensive wardrobe, as befitted a young architect with a substantial income. A final inspection in her full-length mirror convinced Sybil that this was the correct choice for the mediating role she was going to play: no flashiness, just underplayed conservative elegance. It also seemed the right ensemble for St. Honoré's, down to the Hermès scarf. As she left the bedroom, she wondered what Arturo would wear.

Her unconscious preference for an interview suit left her unprepared for what she found. In his champagne-colored linen suit, white open-necked silk shirt and yellowish-tan silk ascot, he might have been cast in a movie as a young Latin lover.

"*Amor,* you look dashing . . ." she started, because it was true. He was a good inch shorter than Sybil, but she loved his taut body and springy gait, his aggressive self-confidence. The carefully trimmed black beard added a seductively demonic touch.

"But?" He moved toward her, with his boxer's step, his left hand gently cupping her chin.

"But nothing, Arturo. It's just . . ."

"Not the right *kohs-tyum* for St. Honoré's?"

Her laugh was slightly forced. "Never mind *le costume*. What about *la cravate*?"

"*No te preocupas, muchacha,*" he replied and kissed her.

Mr. and Mrs. Alan B. Stirling, III, were sitting at a corner table facing the entrance. Mrs. Stirling wore a classic black Chanel suit—the real thing, bought at Bonwit-Teller—a single strand of pearls draped around her neck, and very little makeup. She must have been a striking woman in her youth. Even now, as she approached sixty, there was nothing dowager-like about her tall, trim frame, her creamy skin, her light brown hair and the thick, straight eyebrows that gave her eyes an oriental look.

The maître d', leaning solicitously over her husband's impeccably pin-striped shoulder, was addressing him by name. Alan Stirling expected such recognition, yet he was pleased by it. But the banker's expression changed perceptibly when he caught sight of Sybil, his only daughter, towering—or so it seemed to him—over a miniature, bearded Rudolph Valentino, heading straight toward them. A waiter was trying to stop the young couple but Arturo, with his arm on Sybil's elbow, almost tangoed her to the table before the waiter could intercept this flagrant violator of the restaurant's ties-only dress code.

"Mrs. Stirling, I'm Arturo Flores." Arturo had two ways of pronouncing his name: this time he chose the extra long roll of the *r*. "I've been looking forward to this dinner," he said and kissed her hand. Moving past the stunned maître d' he addressed her husband. "It's very generous of you to join us at St. Honoré's and the theater. I hope you like Lorca."

Both the waiter and the maître d' silently conceded defeat. Sybil was the only one to appreciate the strategy involved in getting around the two tie-policemen and the subtle irony in Arturo's behavior toward her parents. Arturo was no lady's hand-kisser and the delicately balanced Chicano chip on his shoulder generally stopped him from acting deferential toward elder men, especially when he felt he was being subjected to Anglo scrutiny.

Sybil wanted no fencing match and was too independent to be seeking parental approval. She'd made up her mind long ago that Arturo Flores suited her in every respect. She knew that her mother respected her judgment and would support her in any choice pertaining to men. She was less certain about her father: each new beau had to be questioned, tested, judged.

This time, there were two problems she'd never faced before. Arturo had moved in with her, not she with him. Was her father going to think that this man was sponging off a wealthy banker's daughter? The other was his name. Her father claimed not to be prejudiced, and he probably wasn't at his bank; the subject of prejudice probably never arose at the top of the steep pyramid he commanded. But a potential "Sybil Flores"?

Menu in hand, Stirling addressed Arturo. "What will you have to drink?" Without waiting for a response, he turned to the waiter. "I'll have a Campari with soda," he added, "and so will my wife."

"Make it three," interjected Sybil, hoping that Arturo would take the hint.

He didn't. "Nothing right now, thanks. I'll have wine with the meal."

I'll give this point to Daddy, thought Sybil, for whom this dinner had become something of a contest. He had made the bigger effort.

Although this was Arturo's second time at St. Honoré's, he was again shocked by the prices on the menu. Christ, he thought, it's indecent to spend that much on a meal. I guess *el Papa* doesn't care.

The women made their choices and the waiter bowed toward the older man. Instead of ordering, Alan Stirling addressed Arturo. "What are you having, Mr. Flores?"

A nice gesture, not calling him Arturo, thought Sybil, and advanced the score 2–0 in her father's favor.

Arturo had studied the menu as sociological literature, rather than in preparation for a choice. The pompous description of the various items amused him. As he looked up from his menu he realized

approach six hundred dollars, even without the wine or tip. He knew exactly how much the Peter Michael and Palmer bottles cost—and he was the only one of the four who did. Slowly it dawned on him that he might get stuck with the most expensive restaurant meal of his life.

His arithmetic was interrupted by Sybil's father rising from his chair. "Arturo," he said—the younger man's preoccupation with money made him miss the gesture of intimacy, of inclusion into the family—"I'm going to stop at the men's room before we take off for the theater."

As soon as Stirling had departed, Arturo glanced around furtively. Without moving his head, he lifted the edge of the paper resting face down in no-man's land, the way a poker player examines the last card dealt. He dropped it with a shudder when he saw the sum—$1,395.76—but he did have time to wonder about the peculiar seventy-six cents. What the hell, he thought, I might as well test *el padre*. Quickly, he signaled to the waiter, who stood in the distance observing the scene. "Here's my credit card," said Arturo in an uncharacteristically ingratiating voice, "but don't mention that I've already paid for the meal."

As the waiter took the card, he nodded. Had it not been for his self-absorption, Arturo might have noticed the faint smile. But he wouldn't have guessed its cause: three minutes earlier, just around the entrance to the dining room, the waiter had accepted from Alan Stirling sixteen crisp one-hundred dollar bills accompanied by the comment "Keep the change, but don't mention that I've paid the bill."

Arturo Flores was not a stingy man. In fact, within the fairly circumscribed limits of his income, one could call him generous. But spending around fifteen hundred dollars on a dinner for four depressed him. Most of his clients didn't earn that much in a month. As Sybil and her mother returned, she was surprised to see a somber Arturo, chin in hand, staring into space. As far as she could tell, the bill resting on the table was still untouched. Soon they were joined by her father, who promptly startled them with a joke. Sybil was puzzled. Her father wasn't a joke teller. Was this his way of making Arturo feel at ease? If so, her father's behavior had the opposite effect: Arturo's laughter definitely sounded forced. Meanwhile, the bill seemed glued face down to the tray on which it rested, as if invisible to both men. She looked at her watch. In a minute they'd have to leave for the theater. A glance at her mother showed that she'd also noticed the lonely, undisturbed bill. Suddenly, Arturo turned toward her parents. "The theater is only a ten minute walk from here and it's all downhill. If you're willing to walk, we should start."

"A first class idea," exclaimed the father. "It will settle our soufflé. Marian is a great walker, so let's go." His wife gazed at the bill and then at her daughter, who returned the questioning look with a discreet gesture toward the same object, now the centerpiece of the table.

Arturo moved behind Sybil's chair. "*Vámonos*," he whispered with an impatient edge. Marian Stirling, visibly irritated, reached for the bill, but the waiter stopped her. "Excuse me, Madam," he said as he deftly extracted the folded piece of paper from her hand, "This dinner is on the house." Turning to Arturo he added, "What an elegant ascot you're wearing, sir. I should have mentioned it when you first came."

The Psomophile

Even before you heard him speak, it was evident that he was not an American. There were traces of Spanish (*espectacular*, he would say) and on occasion Italian touches, superimposed on Briticisms of the "jolly-bloody-beastly" variety; a good guess might have been an Italian family in South America, say Argentina or Uruguay, who had sent their son to an English school. He wore only custom-made English shoes. His jackets were invariably of Italian design and tight, though not too tight; double-breasted; and made of materials such as checkered cashmere, or Venetian wool, which didn't lose its press even in rain. He now lived in Hillsborough, one of the wealthiest suburbs of San Francisco, and commuted to the city in a chauffeur-driven Jaguar.

But his real mark was his passion for bread. Not all baked goods, and certainly not cakes, but bread—or rolls. Once a friend called him a *paniphile* but he could not accept a bastardized Greco-Latin term. After some debate, they telephoned a Cypriot acquaintance, who narrowed their choices to two. *Artophile* was probably the more correct, based on the ancient Greek *artos* for loaf, but the potential for confusion was bothersome. Of course he was an art lover—one only had to see the walls of his home or office—but ambiguity simply would not do when dealing with bread, and the word *artophile* would sound like another hybrid. *Psomophile* also seemed flawed since the ancient Greeks used *psomos* for a scrap of bread or meat, but their Cypriot, insisting that "*psomi* is the modern Greek for bread," hung up. The word was accepted by the psomophile, who noted that suffering from *psomophilia* sounded deliciously degenerate.

One clear autumn Saturday, the psomophile turned incipient psomomaniac. The man and his wife had been invited to brunch at the home of a Berkeley professor. They arrived late—a Latin habit. Their host led them straight to the buffet table, suggesting that they help themselves before meeting the other visitors. The psomophile also happened to be an admirer of edible art. Not surprisingly, he immediately noticed that the food was already in disarray, but for once he did not mind the violations committed by the earlier guests: the excised truffles from the pâté, the cucumber slice dropped into the hummus, or even the crushed curls of the butter aliquots. His nostrils had started to quiver the way a man's might when he discerns an alluring perfume on a woman. At first sight, the warm round loaf carried by the hostess in a basket might have looked like ordinary hard-crusted, sourdough bread. But to his eyes the imperfections of the bread's surface—the manner in which the edges of the multiple knife slashes tended to sear, or the size of the subcutaneous bubbles of the crust—were unmistakable evidence of a special touch.

There was a component in the aroma that he could not place, that made him salivate. As soon as the hostess had deposited the basket on the table, he headed for it with a serrated bread knife to perform the inevitable ritual: to cut the end piece of the loaf, because it offered the maximum amount of crust, the real proof of a baker's art, and yet enough "flesh" to permit insight into the body of the bread. The moment that he tasted it, he knew. It was Pecorino! Just the slightest trace, but divine! He glanced around and furtively cut the other end of the loaf. He barely noticed the other food he had picked; it was all camouflage for the bread.

Out on the deck he complimented the hostess on her quiche, which he had not yet tasted, and on the bread. "How did you get the idea for the Pecorino taste? So subtle and yet a real signature! Who taught you how to bake such a masterpiece?"

"You're the first to recognize the Pecorino. But I can't take credit for it, I got it from Alessandro's."

"Alessandro's?"

"A local bakery, third-generation Italian, who combine San Francisco sourdough with Italian baking. It's only on Saturdays that they bake this bread."

On the way back, he had little difficulty following her directions to Alessandro's. The display window looked as if it hadn't been washed for days; and except for a few lonely items—a tray containing some rolls, a cake or two—it was empty. But to the seasoned psomophile the bakery looked promising. It was obvious that most goods had been sold and that displaymanship was either unnecessary or scorned by the owner.

A tinny bell rang as he opened the door. After an insolent interval, an elderly man in coat and tie appeared through the rear door. "Yes?" was all he said. The psomophile's request for a loaf of Saturday's special bread produced a snort. "At 1:30?" the baker asked, pointing to the clock on the wall. "We're always sold out by 10:15. We open at ten."

Next Saturday morning at 9:40 a uniformed chauffeur in the psomophile's racing-green Jaguar was parked in front of Alessandro's bakery, reading a newspaper. The display window was fuller than last week but still had not been washed. As the first customers appeared in front of the closed door the chauffeur folded his paper and joined the line. Promptly at ten, the door was unlocked. With hardly an exception, the requests were for "the Special." When the chauffeur ordered five loaves, he was told, "Two to a customer, unless you order ahead of time."

During the next few weeks the chauffeur became a familiar Saturday figure at the bakery. One morning the chauffeur was accompanied by his employer, who made a simple request. "Hold four loaves for me every Saturday, even if the chauffeur is not here by ten. If I want more, I'll order ahead of time." The baker understood a compliment—even one disguised as an order, and especially when the order for a month's supply was paid without demanding a receipt. In return, Alessandro volunteered a piece of information: if frozen promptly, his loaves could be preserved for years, not weeks or months, and would still taste like fresh bread, provided—the right index finger was raised for emphasis—each loaf was defrosted slowly while wrapped tightly in a moist towel. "Slowly," he repeated, his finger jabbing at the cashmere jacked just below the silk handkerchief, "and never heat the bread until it's completely defrosted. And don't re-freeze it."

For the next couple of years, Alessandro's Saturday Special could always be found in the kitchen of the Hillsborough mansion. Usually the psomophile consumed one of the fresh loaves within a few hours of the bread's arrival in his kitchen. The rest was cut into half-loaves, each section wrapped tightly in plastic and frozen. Defrosting by the moist-towel technique worked as promised, but he never tested the "for years" guarantee.

One Saturday, the chauffeur returned with three loaves and the news that Alessandro's bakery would be closed forever. The reasons were mysterious—some of the customers claimed it was loss of the lease, others alluded to a sudden rupture between the elder Alessandro and his son. Whatever the cause, next Saturday was going to be the last day when Alessandro's Special could be purchased.

The psomophile learned from Alessandro over the phone that money was not the problem, that the decision was irrevocable, but that the baker was prepared for a grand gesture, though not the grandest of them all: divulging the recipe for the bread. This was out of the question; he was not even willing to disclose the origin of the Pecorino, except for warning that only one imported brand would do. However, he would accept a special order for one hundred loaves of his bread to be fetched on the last day of his bakery's existence. Alessandro asked only that the Jaguar park in the back alley and not show up until noon. Otherwise, relinquishing one hundred loaves in front of his regular customers that morning would permanently tarnish his reputation for tough even-handedness.

The Jaguar arrived in the alley at 11:50. The psomophile wore a dark blue suit with blue and black striped tie, his version of a mourning suit. Alessandro opened the door the moment the chauffeur and his passenger approached the bakery's rear entrance. Twenty or more white paper bags were stacked against the wall. "You've only got ninety-five loaves here." He had sold out earlier than usual and a couple of his oldest customers were so disappointed that he just didn't have the heart to send them away. "I hope you don't mind. Not that you could do anything about it," he smiled wryly, still calling the shots. The Jaguar's trunk could not cope with all the bread; the overflow rode inside the car and filled it with a strange aroma of Pecorino, British leather, and freshly baked bread.

The chauffeur, the cook, the maid, and the master of the house set to work cutting all but five loaves into three parts, and wrapping each portion tightly in plastic. The five whole loaves were left uncut for a few special events. Only when the bread was ready to be frozen did it dawn on them that 275 parcels, five of them rather bulky ones, would usurp the entire freezer capacity of the kitchen. Without a moment's hesitation the order was issued to remove the current contents of the freezer—pound after pound of steaks, sausages, fish, sweet butter, ice cream, and various unlabeled containers, all dear to the cook. She promptly went to bed, not to reappear until Monday morning.

The psomophile decided to be selfish. With very few exceptions, this bread was to be consumed only by him and his wife, and even they would restrict themselves to one frozen portion per week. Given his frequent travels, the supply was likely to last for at least six years. He refused to worry beyond that time.

This December was one of the wettest months in decades of San Francisco weather records. The torrential rains, spawned by a series of Pacific storms, were accompanied by very high gusts, causing power failures of unprecedented length. San Francisco was relatively unscathed, especially the downtown office and hotel areas. Most of the occupants of these high-rise building were unaware of what was happening just a few miles north, south, and east of the city, where power transmission was largely above ground. Shortly after lunch, the man's secretary interrupted him at a meeting. The note that she presented discreetly referred to a message from his wife, reporting that the electricity in their home had been interrupted since ten in the morning; their dinner was likely to be a cold buffet. "Reserve a suite at the Huntington," he said, "and tell my wife we'll spend the night in the city." Dinner without guests in the city, perhaps followed by a visit to a cinema, was a luxury that both relished but only rarely indulged.

The next morning did not start propitiously. Not only did he have to dress in the same clothes that he had worn the day before, but a dollop of marmalade had landed on his tie to produce the type of sartorial blemish that he would never have tolerated under ordinary circumstances. And then the telephone rang. The maid was calling from Hillsborough to inform his wife that the electric service had still not been restored. What were she and the cook to do about the thawing food in the freezer?

"Oh, forget about it," he said, but before his wife could pass these words on, the enormity of the maid's message sank in: the bread, a minimum of three years' worth of Alessandro's Special. A glance at his pocket diary told him he could head south by 11:00 a.m. Perhaps the insulation of the freezer was such that the bread was still frozen; perhaps the electricity would come on earlier than expected.

The situation was even more serious than he had imagined. On the car radio he learned that crews were coming from as far away as Nevada to help in the repair work; no estimate could be given about the timing of the restoration of electric service. As the chauffeur drove through one of the poorest sections of town on the way to the freeway, past flophouses, run-down hotels, boarded-up buildings, and figures huddled in doorways attempting to keep dry, the psomophile thought morosely about the rapidly thawing, if not totally unfrozen, three years' supply of irreplaceable bread. The prospect of a bread-eating orgy did not console him—where was he going to find forty or fifty guests who'd want to eat bread and cheese in this rain in a dark, cold house? The Jaguar was idling at a traffic light when he saw a line of impoverished men and women pressed against the wall of a building, waiting for the door to open for the free lunch at the San Francisco Gospel Mission.

The rain had stopped in the early afternoon, but a strong wind was still blowing. The latest guesstimate was that electric service would not be restored until midnight at the earliest. The chauffeur and the maid loaded the bread into the trunk of the Jaguar. They had not bothered wrapping 150 odd sections in wet towels—the bread was virtually defrosted before they even departed; it was certain that it would be completely edible by the time they reached the Mission.

The chauffeur was strangely silent as his passenger alluded to Christ and His miracle of the loaves. He couldn't even force a laugh in response to his employer's boast that Alessandro's bread probably tasted better than His. So enamored had the psomophile become of the biblical analogy that he had not given any thought to the impression that his arrival in a Jaguar, chauffeur-driven, would make on Skid Row. The driver, however, had been thinking of nothing else. His worst fears were realized the moment their car pulled up at the converted store front and he saw the dull surprise, mixed with hostility, in the eyes of the people waiting for the opening of the dining room. In addition to the soup kitchen clientele, there were loiterers all down the block. A large proportion of these were black and more gregarious than the people in the waiting line. Many were smoking; two big black men were drinking beer. All stared, and some laughed, as the tall man in the camel-hair coat and the uniformed chauffeur loaded themselves with several white paper parcels each. The men headed through the crowd for the front door, where they found themselves blocked by a nearly toothless old man in dilapidated clothing. "They ain't open until five," he said without moving. The chauffeur looked grimly at his employer, whose sudden helplessness seemed so totally out of character.

"Excuse me, please," mumbled the psomophile as he tried to slide past the old man to the door, only to realize that with his hands full of bread, his feet were the sole available door knocker. A few genteel taps produced no response. Losing all patience, the chauffeur pushed past the old man and repeatedly kicked the door until a thin youth, in blue jeans and gray smock, opened it a crack. "What the hell . . ." he started, but then stopped abruptly as two bags were thrust at him.

"Take these and let us in." The commanding sharpness of these words sufficed for the men's admittance, whereupon the door was slammed before the pushing crowd could follow.

By the time the donation was approved by the kitchen manager and the first load of parcels opened, the chauffeur was perspiring heavily; even his employer showed beads of moisture on his forehead. As they left the dining room for a second load, accompanied by the young man who had opened the door, they found a scene from a postwar movie.

The two black men with their beer were relaxing on the sloping hood of the Jaguar as if on a park bench. Others were leaning against the windows and doors of the car—a human collage on green. Four people, one a spaced-out woman in a torn red ski jacket and purplish woolen cap, were lounging on the trunk of the automobile—its rear window serving as the woman's pillow. The chauffeur didn't even have time to pounce on these exterior passengers. A wave of the young man's hand scattered the motley crew, whereupon the psomophile slid into the car and quickly locked the door.

The chauffeur and shelter attendant moved a second load of bread into the Gospel Mission. They were about to assemble a third batch when the shelter door was unlocked. Immediately, the crowd around the Jaguar thinned as the waiting line of men and women pushed their way into the dining room. Only the two beer drinkers and a few smokers, apparently not regular customers of the soup kitchen, remained around the car. For the first time, the automobile's occupant felt some relief. All he wished now was for the driver's reappearance to implement a rapid departure from such an un-Gallilean environment.

The person bursting out of the dining room, however, was not the chauffeur. The old man, who had initially blocked their way, began to bang his fist on the window of the car. As the psomophile looked at him in astonishment, he spotted the blood trickling out of the old man's open mouth. He recognized, between the man's thumb and index finger, a tooth. Only then did the rush of obscenities reaching him through the protective Jaguar shell make sense: the old man had broken it on the hard crust of Alessandro's Special—probably a bit harder than usual since it had not been defrosted according to the rules, but not too hard for a Hillsborough resident's teeth maintained by semiannual visits to the dentist. Suddenly he realized that what he adored in this bread—the hardy crust, the unusual taste and aroma—might, to the uninitiated brought up on soft white cardboard, suggest spoilage.

The old man threw his tooth at the window, producing a minute and yet distinctly angry-sounding ping against the glass, before rushing back into the dining room. The two beer drinkers on the Jaguar's hood had stopped laughing. For the first time, they showed some interest in one of the soup kitchen's clients. That's when the dining room door broke open again. A small mob, led by the old man with a piece of Alessandro's bread in each hand, stormed towards the car and began to pelt it with bread missiles, the thumps reverberating down the block. The beer drinkers jumped off the hood, leaving their beer cans still resting on it. The woman in the red ski jacket raised one of the intact loaves, and threw it at the door, causing the psomophile inside to duck instinctively. By now, the beer drinkers had decided to make a sport of the debacle. One of the men picked up the round loaf from the gutter and threw it to his companion, who had resumed his seat on the hood as the initial bombardment had slowed down owing to a lack of ammunition. Laughing, the two men passed their bread ball back and forth, back and forth.

The scene lasted only a minute or two. Just as the first wave of assault started its retreat to the dining room, the chauffeur pushed his way through the crowd, quickly unlocked the car, and started the motor. He blew his horn several times but the commanding sound made no impression on the ball player on the hood. Placing the bread loaf between his legs, he leaned forward to face the chauffeur through the windshield. “Drive on, James,” he said, but it was unlikely that the driver heard. What he did catch was an angry growl from the back seat, “Damn you, Lester, get moving.” It was the first time in their eleven years together that the psomophile had cursed his chauffeur.

As the Jaguar crept out of its parking place, the black man on its hood let out a whoop of delight as he raised his bread trophy into the air. Dozens of pedestrians turned; a passing school bus of children screamed with pleasure at the sight. Within fifty yards, the Jaguar came to a stop at a red light, and the human hood ornament jumped off the car. With an elegant, dismissive gesture, he threw the loaf high into the air. It made a loud thud as it hit the Jaguar’s hood, before rolling into the center of the busy street’s traffic. Before the eyes of the passenger and the chauffeur, the loaf was flattened by a passing truck.

The Jaguar shot forward the moment the light turned green. Only then did the passenger notice the bags of bread sitting next to the driver’s seat, the ones that had never been taken into the soup kitchen. A sudden wave of nausea engulfed him; it was clear that he would never be able to touch the last precious crusts of Alessandro’s bread. It was even conceivable that the psomophile would never want to eat bread again.

The Glyndebourne Heist

Name me another opera house where grazing sheep dot the green hills overlooking the place; where the audience, in dinner jackets and evening gowns, arrives from the car park toting chairs, blankets, wicker baskets, and tables that would pass muster in many a dining room; and where some of the real aficionados have already occupied the choice locations—next to the privet hedges or under the huge oaks—to sip champagne and nibble cream cakes, while the cows chew their cud in the adjacent open field across a deep ha-ha.

Glyndebourne is testimony to the British proclivity for pastoral snobbery. It also tests an opera lover's mettle: the long drive or two-hour train and bus ride from London; the need to make reservations months in advance and, for a foreign visitor like me, to be in the country at the right time for the very short season when the summer weather forecasts alternate between "sunny intervals with occasional showers" and "rain at first, sunny intervals developing."

I was myself caught up in the snobbery when I gushed to my host, "Francis, I can't tell you how impressed I am that you managed to get tickets at such short notice." Francis Holbrook—stout, pink-cheeked, and exuding both affluence and power—beamed as he surveyed the scene of bucolic formality. His son, Nigel, aged twenty-two, who'd come down from Cambridge, was sullen. Purposely, we'd arrived early so that they could show me the gardens before the four-thirty curtain call to *Il Ritorno d'Ulisse in Patria.* We were walking down some stone steps towards an oval lawn in front of a pond surrounded by willows and spotted with water lilies. It looked like a favorite site: elsewhere, people kept their distance while they pulled out tablecloths, cutlery and linen napkins; here in the grassy oval, a dozen groups had laid out their stakes in restaurant proximity to each other. "They're sitting here," Nigel muttered, "so they can read the labels of their neighbor's wine bottles."

"What's bothering this misanthrope?" I asked jokingly, addressing the question midway between father and son.

"It offends Nigel's socialist principles," replied Holbrook. "Nigel is probably the only person who's here because of Monteverdi and in spite of Glyndebourne."

"Well, just look at this," growled the son, pointing to a table that might well have been set by a butler. "A *silver* vase with a *yellow* rose! And four *cut* crystal glasses! And *bone china* crockery! And a pepper *mill*! Can you imagine a picnic with an *ordinary* pepper shaker?" The sarcastic emphasis fell like beats of a drum.

"That will do, Nigel," said Holbrook, who had been listening with a bemused smile. It was a warning, not an admonition; at that moment, a tall woman in silver brocade approached the table to rearrange the cutlery. She lifted the second knife at each setting and now placed it in a daring diagonal across the side plate, the tip pointing toward the chair. "Felicity," said a majestic man in evening clothes who was setting down a hamper, "I'll take the caviar out of the cooler. It should be just right at intermission."

"Christ!" growled Nigel. "Let's go in. I can't take any more of this."

At Glyndebourne music yields to gastronomy for the seventy-five minute dinner intermission—one reason why performances start so early. On dry English summer evenings, these formal picnics in the gardens are marvels of sartorial and social decorum. On the more common rainy days, the optimists—the people who had refused to take the precaution of advance bookings at one of the three restaurants on the grounds—withdraw to their automobiles. Then the Daimlers and big Rolls Royces become dining rooms, the Jaguar sports cars and Porsches turn into dinettes.

Francis Holbrook didn't think I should gamble on English weather on my first visit to Glyndebourne. Like other cautious diners, he had ordered the entire three-course meal and wines a week in advance The food was first-rate, the service irreproachable and timed in such a way that even the coffee could be drunk without undue haste before the first warning bell sounded. Nigel, however, excused himself after the *gravlax*, before the boned stuffed quail had even been served. "I hope you don't mind," he announced, "but I'd like to go to into the garden."

Holbrook raised his eyebrows. "The garden? How will you bear the grinding of the pepper mills or the clinking of the glasses?"

"I'll manage," muttered Nigel.

"My son has become the kind of snob you find only in our country," chuckled my host. "He joins the hunt and rides with the hounds, but he wants the fox to win."

Nigel slipped into his seat just as the lights were dimmed for the second act of *Ulisse.* Afterward, in the Bentley, Holbrook remarked, "I say, Nigel, you're suddenly in a very jolly mood. Rather different from how you started out."

His son ignored the comment. "Thanks for taking me along, Father," he said. "It was quite a performance."

"Even the garden scene? Did you become a Tory during intermission? If so, you ought to come back again."

"I might," replied Nigel.

Four days later, to my surprise I received from Nigel a second invitation to Glyndebourne: to *L'Italiana in Algeri.* "We'll pick you up shortly after two; but I must warn you, if the weather is bad, we'll have to postpone it."

In addition to Nigel, "we" turned out to be a young couple in formal evening clothes and the uniformed chauffeur, who was Nigel's age. He was certainly not the man who last week had driven us in the Bentley, but the face looked familiar. It was Cedric, I realized, who had been at the guest seminar that I had given at Cambridge. He had virtually baited me at my talk, which had dealt with entrepreneurship in California's Silicon Valley; "I rather think that we could do without lessons in free-market buccaneering" had been his last snide remark.

"Let me apologize for this mysterious invitation," Nigel was sitting next to Cedric, who was driving the Mercedes station wagon; now he turned to face me. "I wasn't sure you'd accept if I told you about our plan."

"You know how much I enjoyed our last trip to Glyndebourne. And I like youngish company." The moment I had said "youngish," I realized how affected it sounded. "Even if I wanted to, I couldn't change my mind now, at the speed we're traveling."

Nigel didn't smile. "The garden scene at Glyndebourne is a shameful spectacle—the number of people in Britain on the dole is going through the roof; all those millions starving in Africa; and these characters in black tie . . ."

"And the evening dresses," inserted Pippa Stanley-Hunter, the bosomy brunette on my right, wearing a spectacularly décolleté gown. "All of them act as if nothing had changed in the last fifty years."

"Come off it, Nigel," I said, "Glyndebourne isn't all that bad. Besides, Africans don't like caviar."

"Very funny," replied Nigel.

I glanced at Pippa, but her pained expression made her loyalties clear. "Go on," I said, in no mood for dialectics.

Nigel hesitated, then bribed me with a smile. "This isn't the place for sociopolitical discussions. Besides, both you and Dad are hopeless. We invited you because we need somebody respectable looking and not too young."

"Thanks," I said, wryly.

"Just a statement of fact," added Pippa.

"Did you notice the four hampers behind you?" asked Nigel.

"Yes. And why do we need four huge baskets for one opera intermission? You could feed dozens of starving . . ."

"Derek, why don't you open them?" Nigel's interruption ended my attempts at social commentary. I was getting curious: what did they really want from me?

The young man on my right turned around and lifted the cover of the container nearest him. It was empty.

"There's nothing in it" I exclaimed.

"Right. Now open the next one," ordered Nigel.

Derek reached farther back and flipped open the top of the second hamper, revealing several bottles of grape juice.

"Go on, Derek. Show him the pita slices and the hummus, but note how discretely they're packaged."

"For heaven's sake, Nigel," I said. "So we're going to do penance for the culinary excesses of all the other people at Glyndebourne? You've got enough juice for all of us and then some!"

It turned out that there was only one opera ticket—even that had been difficult to get—but a flash of the envelope was enough to get us past the attendant into the car park. Cedric, in chauffeur's livery, was ignored completely as he carried one of the hampers to the spot Nigel had selected the week before. On one side we were sheltered by a hedge, yet we were within easy sight and hearing of the oval picnic area that was so popular. While Nigel walked with me through the gardens—so we would be seen together by as many people as possible—the others removed the blankets from the hamper and arranged the four picnic settings. When we returned, Derek was sitting on the blanket, his elbow on the closed hamper, surveying the scene. Pippa was sipping wine. Nobody would've guessed that the wine was a cheap Bulgarian Cabernet Sauvignon, the current "in" drink at Cambridge, or that under the debonair aloofness of this handsome couple seethed thoughts of crushing unemployment in Liverpool and bloated bellies in the Sudan.

"Let's go," announced Nigel. "When we get to the tennis court, you turn left toward the auditorium with the rest of the crowd, while we head for the car. We'll wait there until the performance has started. Cedric will take the next hamper out and fiddle around like somebody's chauffeur till he's sure everyone is inside, and then he'll get us. We'll fetch the other hampers. Between us we ought to finish everything in just a few minutes."

I was amazed how cool they were. But why not? They fitted so perfectly into the Glyndebourne milieu—dress, accent, bearing. No wonder British spies like Guy Burgess remained undetected for so long. But what about me? Did I look as conspicuous as I felt? I didn't remember ever having worn a tuxedo in the middle of the afternoon, and here I was in a rented one for the second time in a week. I wasn't even certain of my role. Witness? Co-conspirator? Or just a prop? We were practically at the tennis court when Nigel turned to me, for the first time sounding anxious.

"You've got an aisle seat. Please leave the moment the curtain falls and hurry to our picnic site. Start taking out some of the food from the hamper—at least the smoked salmon—and put it on the plates.

We'll come as soon as the rest of the crowd moves across the lawns. Thanks and good luck."

Good luck? I mused. Had I just been promoted? But so far I hadn't done anything and I didn't intend to. People would see me inside at the opera—there'd be no way that I could be implicated, I hoped. Still, I had agreed to go along.

I wasn't the only one to skip the first act curtain call of Elvira, Isabella, and Mustafa. Some members of the Glyndebourne audience always duck out before the lights go on—delegated by friends, wives, or parents to run to the car for the missing delicacies, or to open the wine bottles so that the claret has a chance to breathe. Still, I was one of the first to reach our section of the garden and like a veteran Glyndebourner I opened our hamper, the one that Derek had not shown me in the car. Now I understood the reason: the thinly cut, pale pink, smoked salmon most certainly didn't come from a proletarian grocery store, nor did the Strasbourg goose liver pâté with truffles. I had barely arranged the salmon slices on the plates when Nigel and his two friends arrived.

"Toss the salad, darling," said Derek as he handed the long fork and spoon to Pippa. "I'll handle the wine."

"Where is Cedric?" I asked. "What's he eating?"

"Hummus on pita," grinned Nigel. "Surely, we can't have the chauffeur eat here."

"I've only had time to take out the smoked salmon and the pâté," I said.

"I hope you noticed it had truffles," interrupted Derek. "I robbed the family pantry."

"So I did. And I haven't even opened some of the other packages. But I did see the Fortnum & Mason labels, you parlor socialists."

Nigel tapped me gently on the hand with the long baguette which he was in the process of breaking into four pieces. "Don't touch them yet," he grinned. "They're for later. Just trifles, so to speak."

"I presume we're all eating for the sake of authenticity rather than socialist principles." One of my habits is to hide discomfort behind banter.

"Precisely," replied Nigel.

"Oh, look! Quick! There it starts," Pippa whispered. "The table just to the right of the woman in green. I knew this was going to be a good lark."

I didn't have the faintest idea which dinner groups they had picked but I should have realized that the smallish oval would be a prime target, since the diners at their tables or on the blankets were so close together. Perhaps it was my unconscious guilt that had made me sit with my back towards that area: if I couldn't see those people, they couldn't see me. . . .

Pippa went on, *pianissimo.* "They're the ones with the Beaujolais. I figured anybody cheap enough to drink that stuff might as well get the grape juice. Look how he's talking to his wife; she's got to be his wife, otherwise she wouldn't pretend nothing was wrong." She leaned forward to stifle her laughter. "Look how she's pouring! As if it were exactly what they'd intended to have all along: grape juice in cut crystal! I might as well tell you," she dropped her voice even further, "their Beaujolais went to the couple sitting on the blanket just below the bloke looking at his juice. I exchanged it for their Château Talbot, which is now back with Cedric in the car. Nigel, I can't keep staring at them; but do tell me when they realize it."

The excitement of my companions was infectious; I almost felt like a participant. "Let's see," said Nigel, who had put on mirrored glasses in spite of the fact that the sun had already set. He seemed to have thought of everything. I hate those glasses, where you can't see the other person's eyes; instead you catch your own distorted image in miniature. But they were ideal for his purpose. "He's opening one of the bottles. It's wrapped in a napkin . . ."

"I did that," Pippa expressed her triumph *sotto voce.* "I figured he'd miss the Beaujolais label."

"Splendid!" Nigel's two blank mirrors pointed in the direction of the impending disaster. "He's pouring some in his glass . . . he's lifting it . . . it's at his lips. . . ." Nigel raised his own glass to act out his patter.

"Somebody tell me what's going on," I demanded.

Nigel motioned with his hand, a muffled "wait!" keeping me in suspense. "He's unfolding the napkin. . . ."

Even with my back toward the scene, I could hear the bellowed "Bloody awful Beaujolais! Who in blazes brought this stuff?" I had to turn around. What I saw was a farcical tableau by Feydeau: the outraged Beaujolais taster on the blanket—his Château Talbot palate violated; the ex-Beaujolais owner sitting just above him, a wine glass full of grape juice in his hand, the slow recognition of infamy spilling over his face; and the rest of the crowd—the men in black, the women competing in color with the flowers—startled by decibel levels usually heard only inside the auditorium, not in this most English of English garden settings.

"Nigel," broke in Pippa, "which table did you favor with the hummus?"

"None here. I took that hamper to the other side of the hedge." He rose from the blanket. "This general had better inspect that battlefield."

"I say, those four over there do have style." Derek was pouring himself some more of the Bulgarian wine. Now he pointed behind me. "They had a top notch basket: a big tin of real Beluga caviar and the best wine of the lot. The two bottles of the '76 Latour each will bring at least three hundred quid at the auction."

"Auction?" I had barely adjusted to my status as an innocent participant in a risky escapade, when the ante was again being raised. "What auction?"

I didn't like the complacency in his face. "You think it rather beastly of us not to have told you earlier, don't you? I hope you didn't think we were thieves. We're the modern Robin Hoods of Glyndebourne: we're organizing a fancy-food auction at Cambridge . . ."

"Derek, let me guess," I interrupted. "With the proceeds from the caviar and the wines and all the other loot you'll buy corn and wheat for Africa."

Derek raised his glass and winked. "What I left them instead was the cheapest Chianti we could find and some of those bright red salmon eggs—a huge glass jar. They can't miss it. But look at them. I thought they'd be bloody angry, but they seem to be having an outrageous time. The man with the waxed mustache has been pouring the wine as if it were the best claret in the world—he's even wrapped a napkin around it. And *he* did it," Derek was addressing Pippa, "not I. I wanted to be damn sure he would see the Chianti label, although the shape of the bottle alone would've told him this was no Chateau Latour. Look how she's laughing with that big spoon full of red goo. If they're snobs, at least they've got a sense of humor. Or maybe they're actors!"

From the distance, I saw Nigel approaching. He seemed disappointed. There was nothing Robin-Hoodish in his demeanor. After sitting down, he started to play with the trifle in his dish, which we had filled during his absence.

"What's the report from the hummus and pita front?" When Nigel didn't reply, Pippa prompted once more. "Well?"

He shrugged his shoulders. "I'll tell you later."

I was getting a bit tired of the joke, although I'd been laughing along with the three of them. It was time to stretch my legs before the start of the second act. "We'll wait for you in the car," called Nigel as I headed for the formal flower garden.

The first burst of applause following the final septet had just broken out. I was waiting for Frederica von Stade to make her curtain call; she'd sung a superb Isabel, and the opera's spaghetti scene had been greeted by the audience with uproarious laughter. I stayed until the very last *brava.* As I pushed my way through the crowd, I saw Nigel waving at me.

"You didn't have to come for me," I said. "I remember where the car was parked."

"That's not why I'm here," he replied a bit sheepishly. "We have another passenger in the car. Please don't bring up our prank with the food."

"How did you end up with another passenger?" I asked.

"Wait 'til we get out," said Nigel as he led the way toward the tennis courts.

I still can't fathom how our hamper had pita bread and hummus and those Cox's Orange Pippin apples," said Millicent. I never did hear her last name when we exchanged introductions in the car, nor did I catch a good look at the young woman as I climbed into the Mercedes. All I got were flash exposures of her left profile—the curly dark hair, pudgy nose and slightly protruding teeth—from the occasional headlights of oncoming traffic. This time, Derek was driving, Nigel in the seat next to him, the two women and I in the back seat, and Cedric stretched out behind us among the four food baskets. "And it came from Harrods," she added in a plaintive voice.

"Did you see them pack the basket?" asked Pippa.

"No. I called Harrods from the office. Mr. Shaw only invited me the day before, when a Japanese client of the firm canceled his trip."

"Was Shaw the grim man sitting at your table and staring at the crowd?" asked Nigel.

"He was bloody angry when he opened the brand new wicker basket. I also got it at Harrods—I believe it's called 'the Glyndebourner.'"

A muffled "You don't say!" could be heard from the front.

"I guess Mr. Shaw wasn't talking to me anymore when you saw us." It was clear that Millicent hadn't caught the sarcasm in Nigel's voice. "He's a bit stiff in the office, but he's a fair boss, and you can't really blame him. I didn't believe it at first when he told me I could spend a couple of hundred quid for the hamper and food. Mr. Shaw isn't usually much of a spendthrift. But then he explained all about Glyndebourne and how his Japanese guest would never forget it . . ."

"Still, it was pretty mean to blame you," said Pippa. "Harrods obviously made a mistake when they filled your hamper."

"You should've heard the Harrods food consultant they put on the phone when I explained I was ordering a basket for Glyndebourne and wanted some advice. I've never eaten quail eggs in aspic; I don't even know what the dish looks like. And the caviar—I don't believe you can guess what a small tin costs. Or maybe you can; you've probably drunk the champagne they recommended. Moët," she added, putting the emphasis on the first syllable. "I can still hear the way the gentleman from Harrods described the sweets: 'profiteroles stuffed with heavy pastry cream and smothered with ripe strawberries.'"

"Well, maybe somebody in the shipping department did it for a lark."

"For a lark?" Millicent sounded indignant.

"Maybe it wasn't a lark," interjected Nigel. "Perhaps it was a protest."

"Against what?"

"Why, against all the waste and ostentatiousness of these Glyndebourne intermission feasts."

"I rather fancied it and I didn't see much waste. And what did you people eat?"

I decided it was time to come to Nigel's rescue. I owed it to him for *L'Italiana.* "How did you end up with us here in the car? What happened to your Mr. Shaw?"

Nigel took over immediately. "The prig abandoned her! When I came by the second time, after all the people had left for the next act, I saw Millicent alone; she was sobbing. I told her we didn't have tickets and were just accompanying you to the opera. I felt she might as well return with a more sympathetic crowd than that grouch Shaw."

"It's such a shame. This was my first opera and I don't even know how it ended." So far Millicent had ignored me completely, but now she addressed me. "You saw it all. What happened in the second act?"

"It ends with one of the funniest scenes in opera," I started, without thinking. "You remember in the first act how Mustafa, the Bey of Algiers, falls in love with his Italian captive, Isabella, who in turn is in love with the Bey's slave, Livorno?"

"Lovely, wasn't it?" She nodded.

"Well, in the second act, Isabella dupes Mustafa by cooking a huge dish of spaghetti with tomato sauce and cheese. She grates the parmesan while singing in full voice, and then escapes with her lover because Mustafa is totally preoccupied with the first spaghetti he has ever seen."

"God, I'm hungry," she sighed. "I could even eat fish and chips. I didn't have any lunch—I was saving myself." She gave a hollow laugh.

"Crawl back here with me," said Cedric. "We've got plenty of food left. You'll have to take potluck, though; it's dark back here." His last words hung tumescently in the silent car.

Cedric had hardly finished with his invitation; he was till pushing the baskets around to create additional room while Millicent was already clambering over the back seat. "Come, sit over here," murmured Cedric. "I'll open the basket and you just reach in."

After some giggling, we heard Millicent's disappointed voice. "Stilton! It's the one cheese I don't fancy."

"Never mind, there's lots of stuff here. Let me see what I find. Try this," he said after a pause. "It's soft and it doesn't smell of cheese. In fact, I can't smell anything through the paper. Better use a spoon."

I could hear the rustle of paper and the subsequent purr of delight. "Ah, this is better, much better. Cedric, take a bite and tell me what you think it is."

"Squishy eggs," he said laughingly, his mouth still full.

"You're right," she exclaimed "But what kind?"

"Maybe it says on the wrapper," suggested Cedric.

I could see Nigel's instinctive gesture, but it was too late for any warning. Millicent had flipped on the inside-light switch.

"Why . . ." she commenced and then stopped abruptly. I had turned around just in time to see her rummage through the other packages. "You bloody bastards," she screeched. "So *you* did it!" And with that cry the bombardment started.

The first missile, the quail eggs nested in aspic, hit Nigel on the shoulder. The next one, the profiteroles, shot past me to splatter against the inside windshield.

"For Christ's sake, stop it," exclaimed Derek as he slammed on the brakes. "I can't see." But it was too late. He swerved onto the shoulder of the road and sideswiped a post bearing an RAC emergency telephone.

I was thrown against the back of Nigel's seat. He and Derek jumped out of the car and raced around to open the back of the estate wagon. But the interval was sufficient for the enraged Millicent to empty the remainder of her dinner basket all over the car. I only saw the cover of Harrods special mango chutney being ripped off and the contents poured over Pippa's back and bare shoulders. As she lurched forward, the mess slid down between her breasts like lava.

Millicent climbed out of the back, her hands dripping, the front of her dress like a painter's pallet. "You poncey little Cambridge shits," she shouted, tearful, and stalked off toward the distant lights of a petrol station.

I was the last one out. My head was starting to ache and as I touched my forehead, I felt a sticky ooze. Cautiously I got out of the car and approached Nigel, whose starched white shirt looked blood-spattered from the strawberries. He pointed at the smashed front grill and the huge dent in the left fender.

"Christ," he muttered. "How am I going to explain that one to my father?"

"Nigel," I said, "could you help me? I think I'm bleeding."

He glanced at me quickly and then leaned forward, his eyes narrowing, as if he wanted to get me into sharper focus.

"You'll be OK," he said, and started to rummage in his pockets. I thought that he was searching for a handkerchief to wipe off the blood which had started to run into my eyes. Instead he produced a comb, made of tortoise shell with silver trimming on top and one side. "Here, comb the caviar out of your hair."

The Futurist

"I have nine fifty . . . one million one . . . one million two in the aisle . . . three in the center of the room . . . one point four against you, sir. Say one five? Yes? Fair bid, one five . . . one five . . . one five." The auctioneer scanned the room one last time. The 1912 Boccioni was a powerful painting and a large one at that—at least four feet by six. But 1.5 million pounds sterling? thought Donna Massingham. It had taken less than a minute to reach this record for an Italian Futurist, at which point only three bidders remained. One was a telephone caller, communicating with the auctioneer via a prim young woman on the podium, phone in hand. Another was in one of the front rows; Donna couldn't make him out, she was too far back, but she could see his paddle popping up from time to time. It seemed like bad manners compared to those of the third competitor. He was sitting somewhere nearby—she could see the auctioneer's eyes hover in her neighborhood each time the bid was raised. He must be one of those mystery buyers, Donna thought, who tweaks his left ear lobe or scratches his right nostril—each tweak or scratch worth four years' tuition in an Ivy League college.

Donna's present position as assistant curator at the museum did not cover acquisitions, but she loved to attend auctions in her specialty—early twentieth-century European art. She'd been to Sotheby's and Christie's many times, but always in New York. Now she was attending her first London auction and admiring the low-key, Oxbridge manner in which the man on the podium—really one's image of a banker—conducted the affair. The last "one five" had been accompanied by a nod in the direction of the woman holding the telephone, indicating that the top bid was currently somewhere abroad. The auctioneer peered over his glasses at the front row, but no hand was waved this time. His lips had parted to announce for the final time the winning bid, when just the faintest smile appeared on his face. Before the exultant "one six" had registered on the audience, the woman on the phone was whispering. She hung up as the auctioneer glanced at her. The Boccioni had been sold for 1,600,000 pounds, not counting the substantial sales commission.

"Isn't that something?" Donna said aloud, to nobody in particular. "Almost two and one-half million dollars for this Boccioni."

The man on her right, whom she had not noticed before, turned to her. "You don't think it's worth it?"

"Just look at the pre-sale estimate." She pointed to the open catalogue in her lap.

"It happens all the time," retorted the man, "when two collectors want the same lot and can afford it. But this is a rare one; the woman's head could've been painted by one of the Paris cubists. It really ought to hang next to Picasso's portrait of Ambroise Vollard. But it won't." He chuckled.

"Do you know who got the Boccioni?" asked Donna.

"I even know the wall on which it will hang after it's been reframed." It was the beginning of a conversation that eventually led Donna's neighbor to invite her to visit his private art collection near Milano when he learned that she was heading for an art vacation in Italy.

Donna's eyes were adjusting from the Italian sunshine to the subdued light coming through the French windows. Direct sunlight was never permitted to shine into the high-ceilinged room where they were sitting on an eighteenth-century sofa. Two matching upholstered chairs and two side tables, covered with stacks of gallery announcements, art magazines, and auction catalogues completed the sparse furnishings. Sparse, that is, if one didn't count the paintings on the walls, or the Plexiglas cubes scattered throughout the room which made the sculptures on them seem to be floating in air.

When August Himmelschwanz said, "Call me Gus," Donna had been placed in a special class—the Americans whom Himmelschwanz wanted to impress. At home, in Düsseldorf, he was usually "Herr Generaldirektor." On his estate in Northern Italy, which housed his collection of Italian Futurists, he was "Augusto" to his carefully selected circle of Italian admirers. To occasional British visitors, like Sir Hugh Eckersley, who had written *the* major English text on the Futurists, he was simply "Himmelschwanz." It sounded like a curse when bellowed by Sir Hugh in his *basso profundo.*

The moment Himmelschwanz had learned at the London auction that Donna was a museum curator—the "assistant" in her official title might have cost her the invitation—and that Italy was part of her holiday itinerary, he suggested that she inspect his collection. Ten days later, she arrived in a rented Ford Fiesta, and now he was "Gus" and she "Donna."

They'd been wandering in the gardens surrounding his seventeenth-century Italian villa, now known as Villa Cielo. Entering through the French windows, they had finally reached his favorite place: the first-floor drawing room containing some of the fruits of what he called his "didactic collecting." This majestic room—perhaps forty-five or more feet long from entrance door to French windows, and some twenty feet wide—housed the gems of Himmelschwanz's collection of early Futurists. It was the room where the Boccioni would hang once it arrived from London and had passed through the hands of the Milano establishment that did all of Himmelschwanz's framing.

Shortly after he had acquired the mansion, Himmelschwanz had all the electric fixtures ripped out. He was not interested in candelabra or other ornate lamps; only the most modern track lighting system with dimmable spotlights would do for his Villa Cielo. Cesare Villotti, the village electrician, had become almost a full-time employee of the Himmelschwanz establishment. He had been called many times to make alterations: installing a dimmer; adding another track; replacing some of the spotlights; and helping with the perpetual rehanging of the pictures. Himmelschwanz insisted on himself making all decisions pertaining to the correct illumination of his collection, and on being present whenever a painting was hung or a sculpture positioned. Cesare Villotti was like a village doctor who had to respond at the oddest hours to any summons from the local manor house. Whenever Himmelschwanz bought a new painting, or loaned one out to some museum, Villotti was summoned to help in the rearrangement of the wall space and lighting.

Cesare knew nothing about modern art, but he was proud of the Italian names that he read on the labels: Severini, Prampolini, Russolo. And in Himmelschwanz's presence, Cesare was deeply conscious of being Italian. In his early twenties, he had spent several years in Switzerland as a *Gastarbeiter.* He'd learned very early, and especially on lonely weekends, that this term was a euphemism for "second-class foreigner." He had never lost his sensitivity toward the disdain that many Swiss and Germans showed for foreign workers, especially the southern Europeans.

And he never let on that he understood German. Many times, Cesare would be standing on a ladder fiddling with the lights, while Himmelschwanz informed some visitor in German as to why one could not really depend on the locals: they were charming, simple folk; they had a sense of humor; he loved their songs, but when it came to reliability . . .

More than once Cesare had been tempted to climb down the ladder and walk out, with his middle finger stuck up in the classic Italian gesture. "Screw that damned bulb in yourself . . . and screw you." But he always resisted the temptation when he remembered what an enviable sinecure his Villa Cielo position really was.

Himmelschwanz gave the dimmer a half turn. The works were not arranged by artists' names, but grouped by style. The wall facing the sofa seemed to Donna designed to illustrate the similarity and divergence between the Paris Cubists and the Italian Futurists. There was another Boccioni of 1912, a Carlo Carra of the same year, a very early Prampolini, a Soffici with Cubist overtones. Among these, in the very middle of the long wall, hung two Cubist oils by Picasso or Braque, which seemed virtual copies.

When Cesare Villotti had suggested to his employer that separate dimmers for two paintings hanging right next to each other, and furthermore nearly identical, was a waste of money, he received his first and only art lecture. It was precisely because they were so similar, yet painted by two of the giants of the twentieth century, that they had to be capable of being lit separately. Moreover, it amused Himmelschwanz to have his visitors guess which was the Picasso and which the Braque. By playing with the lights he could focus their attention first on one and then the other.

"*Signore*," Villotti had asked, "could you have told them apart? I don't see any signatures."

"They left them unsigned, deliberately. But all you'd have to do is look at the back." It was not an invitation to lift them off the wall; it was simply a statement of fact.

"But you, *Signore*, now that you've had them for a while, can you tell which is which?"

Himmelschwanz shrugged. "If I study them very carefully, yes. But I don't need to. The Picasso is always on the right. I never change these two."

"Hmm," was Villotti's sole response. Later on, when he'd completed the final adjustment of the lights and the owner had departed, he lifted first one and then the other painting from their hooks to inspect the collage of museum labels on the back of each picture. "Hmm," he said again, this time to himself.

The cook and maid are both off today," Himmelschwanz said. "Why don't you look around while I make some coffee?"

Donna headed straight for the two oils in the center of the room. For her they were like old friends; her graduate thesis had dealt with the Cubists. By the time her host had returned, she was in a corner inspecting a 1914 ink drawing by Giacomo Balla that she would never have recognized had it not been for the carefully printed label.

She accepted the proffered cup of coffee. "It's simply breathtaking," she said. "Now I understand why you had to get that Boccioni in London."

Himmelschwanz's look bordered on the ecstatic. Compliments by art professionals meant much more to him than the effusions, tinged with envy, that he received from fellow collectors.

"But tell me," she continued, "where did you get that Picasso on the left, next to the Severini?"

"Are you sure that's a Picasso?"

Donna caught the sly note in the question. "I'd be willing to bet it is. I just looked at it."

"Would you really?'

"What I mean is—I'm certain about the Picasso. But no, I wouldn't bet with you. First of all, how could I bet with my host about something when I know ahead of time I'd win? Wouldn't that be ungracious?"

"Any other reason why you wouldn't bet?" he persisted.

"Well, we aren't in the same league when it comes to betting, are we, Gus?" Donna blushed when she realized that she had actually taken him up on his "Call me Gus" invitation.

Himmelschwanz seemed too excited to notice. His eyes swept the room "Do you see that painted teapot over there, next to the wooden flowers?" He pointed to one of the Plexiglas cubes in the room. "Do you know whose they are?"

Donna had caught the patronizing implication of the question. She wished she could have put him in his place. "No," she conceded, "I don't."

"Which do you like better?'

"The teapot," she said. "It's really quite handsome. Who did it?"

"Balla. He did these in the twenties—painted wooden flowers, furniture, ceramics. Here, I'll bet you this teapot that the painting on the left," he stressed the last word, "is not by Picasso. You wanna bet?"

Donna smiled politely at the clumsy Americanism. "But what could I bet in return?" She had no idea of the value of Balla's ceramic, except that almost anything of his was likely to cost at least several thousand dollars. She got up from the sofa; Himmelschwanz had sounded so cocksure. But no—the Picasso was hanging on the left.

"Isn't the teapot good enough?" he asked. "Or have you changed your mind?"

"If you mean about the Picasso, no. I haven't changed my mind. But I have nothing to offer in exchange for this Balla."

"I know something that you can offer me—in the unlikely event that you lose." My God, she thought, so that's it? And here we are out in the sticks, the servants gone.

But Himmelschwanz continued, "I've decided that the time has come to prepare a complete catalogue of my collection and I'd prefer it to be in English. I've been looking around for somebody who'd undertake the job. How about it? If you lose the bet, you'll write the catalogue. Of course, not gratis."

Donna's face at that moment should have been painted by a Futurist—someone like Balla, who had been infatuated by movement and change; as in his speeding car paintings, a masterful example of which was hanging in this room. Her initial fear had changed to relief, then surprise, and finally conviction.

"All right . . ." she said, after a pause. "Who's going to settle who won?"

"You will," he said. "Just lift the painting off the wall and look at the labels on the back. There must be at least half a dozen—including one from Christie's, where I bought it." He leaned back in the sofa. "Go on. Lift it off the hook," he coaxed.

To Donna Massingham he looked the way one of her professors had during the final exam for her thesis, after having thrown her a tricky question. Seeing his learned smirk dissolve into politeness when he heard her answer had been delicious.

In measured steps she reached the wall and removed the painting on the left. She did not allow herself a glow. She walked to the sofa, the painting hanging by its wire on her two middle fingers, and handed it, face up, to Himmelschwanz.

He didn't look at it or turn it over. He acted like a poker player holding a royal flush who didn't even ask to see his opponent's hand. "The Braque can fool you," he began, consolingly.

"Not really," replied Donna. She lifted the lid of the Balla teapot and peered inside. "It's never been used, has it?"

What's Tatiana Troyanos Doing in Spartacus's Tent?

Through years of sexual reality, I dreamed ever so often of a woman lover who'd sing while coupling with her man. Once a husky-voiced woman, who'd brought her guitar, started to sing in a stunning contralto. Lying on my bed, exhausted and content, gazing at the naked woman strumming her instrument, I was about to ask her whether she could. . . . But then I chickened out; I was afraid she'd just laugh.

Years later, I happened to go to a performance of Monteverdi's *L'incoronazione di Poppea*, set in the time of Emperor Nero before he went mad, with Tatiana Troyanos singing the lead role. About half-way through the love scene on the couch between young Nero and Poppea, the performance assumed such erotic overtones that I began to squirm in my seat. I don't go to operas for sexual titillation; except for an occasional *Salome* or *Lulu*, it's the music that excites me. But this was different. Suddenly I realized that Troyanos was the woman of my fantasies who had walked into Spartacus's tent over two thousand years ago.

I was a relatively late bloomer, a virgin until nearly twenty. But as an otherwise precocious teenager, I made up for it soaking in the delicious warmth of a full bath. Not in one of those modern tubs, where even I—only five foot five—can't stretch out, so shallow that the water barely reaches one's navel, where either shoulders or feet project into the cold. No, my passions throve in a real tub—one of those huge prewar jobs—where I'd float, water up to the chin, with soapy hands between my thighs, incandescently copulating with Veronica Thwale.

When I met that cool, severely dressed, sexual androgyne—perfumed in civet and flowers, walking down a church aisle, the *Decameron* camouflaged inside the covers of her prayer book to prove the pleasures of blasphemy—I was smitten for weeks, then months. Veronica, in her twenties, was the deftly cunning courtesan I'd been waiting for and had finally found: in Aldous Huxley's *Time Must Have a Stop*. God, she was something! Once our passion slipped me forward in that six-foot tub, so that I choked on soapy water.

But the spur to my longest and most lucid dream was *The Gladiators*—Arthur Koestler's version of the slave uprising led by Spartacus. Don't get me wrong: as time passed, as I became a man, there were months, even whole years, when Spartacus did not exist. But the vision never departed totally from my memory. When I had a lover whose climax always ended in such a long-drawn cry that we could never meet in a hotel, I wondered more than once how Spartacus had handled this in his tent on the plains of Campania. And when I saw Yury Grigorovich's choreography of *Spartacus* at the Bolshoi in Moscow thirty-five years after I'd read Koestler's novel, I felt a pleasure reawakening.

I still remember where the scene appeared: on a left-hand page, fairly high up, three or four lines from the top. Koestler had sketched Spartacus's portrait with just a few deft strokes: the tall, slightly hunched body draped with fur-skin; his wandering eyes and cleverness; his freckles; his words that seared your ears as he spoke. And the women he had come to his tent to satisfy his sexual urges—the camp-followers, the *impedimenta.* But one evening, on that left-hand page, a woman of a different breed came to him. I, the teenage virgin, saw it clearly: the tent flap swaying as she slid in barefoot; a whiff of musk and ointment and female sweat entering with her; the chocolate skin gleaming as she passed the flickering candle; her firm breasts bearing nipples like diamonds on a ring. She kneeled beside Spartacus's reclining figure, peeled off his fur-skin and wordlessly started to caress him. For once, Spartacus took no initiative; he let the woman pleasure him. When she saw him aroused, she proceeded to sing in a low voice, mounting him—the first time Spartacus had ever been mounted by a woman—and with his phallus deep in her, she thrust faster and faster, singing more loudly, in full voice, to her climax. I know what you're thinking. But remember, I'd read Koestler's novel well over half a century ago as an innocent youth who wanted to have his fur-skin removed.

Since *Poppea*, I saw Troyanos in many roles, from a very male Julius Caesar in Handel's opera, or a flighty Dorabella in *Cosi Fan Tutte*, to a concert performance in Berlioz's *Les Nuits d'Eté.* At the end of the Berlioz, I met one of the musicians, whom I knew quite well, and told him how touched I'd been by Troyanos's singing. On the spur of the moment I spilled out the Koestler story—he's the only person who's heard it—and confessed that in Troyanos's Poppea I had finally seen the woman of my bathtub days. I even alluded to my most recent Troyanos fantasy: listening to her while we're both soaking in a hot tub. That's when he caught me by surprise. Did I want to meet Troyanos? he asked; he could arrange an introduction. "Absolutely not," I replied. He seemed taken aback, so I tried to explain that a life-long illusion might be destroyed. What if, screwing up my courage, I blurted out my Spartacus tale to Troyanos and asked, "Do you sing when you make love?" She'd probably fix me with those huge dark eyes, this time full of impishness and irony, and murmur, "Don't all women?" What then? Would I've dared to mention my choice of the song I wanted to hear as she . . . ?

Instead, I went home and decided to reread *The Gladiators*, which I hadn't looked at for decades. But I couldn't even find the book; I must have lost my copy during one of my many moves. The local library didn't have it. Finally I located a worn copy at the university, a 1950 third printing by Macmillan. I took the volume home and skimmed the upper portions of the left-hand pages. That probably took half an hour, because every once in a while I stopped to read a choice paragraph or two. But I was so impatient to find my scene that I kept turning the pages. I found nothing. Well, I figured, maybe this edition is printed in a different format. Back I went to page one and flipped through the right-hand pages. Again, nothing. It was preposterous. I'd seen Troyanos in *Poppea* and everything in me—memories of untold and untellable fantasies, embellished by the wishful inventions of late middle age—told me that she'd been in Spartacus's tent. I was prepared to concede minor imperfections in my memory; but the fact that she had mounted Spartacus and sung, *that* simply had to be there.

So I took the book to bed and read it, slowly, starting with the prologue: *It is night still. Still no cock had crowed.* It's a great beginning and I savored every page. That is, every page until I got to page 84—a left-hand page. There in lines twelve to fourteen Koestler has Spartacus say these words to Crixus: "I have never been to Alexandria. It must be a very beautiful place. Once I lay with a girl, and she sang. That is what Alexandria must be like."

I've never been to Alexandria and I've never lain with an Egyptian woman. But no temptation on earth would cause me to do so now. Instead, I tore out page 84. "Damn you, Arthur Koestler," I muttered as I shredded it into illegibility. "Damn you."

The Toyota Cantos

I still think it's absurd. There I was in the hospital, my arm in a cast, feeling sorry for myself, and still not knowing precisely how I'd smashed up Bea's car. According to the police, it was a virtual wreck. They just towed it to the dump. So what did I do? I didn't even wait to get home. I called my wife in Paris. "Bea," I said. Or maybe it was *Bay-ah-tree-chay*, which under the circumstances was clearly a mistake. The first time I pronounced her name that way was at a departmental party when I was still an assistant professor. She just laughed. I guess she was humoring the budding Dante scholar. The next time around, she responded with a faint smile, but after that she just looked pained. Once, a couple of years later, she blew up: "Goddamit, Lionel, you just married me so you could demonstrate that, like, Dante, you had a *Bay-ah-tree-chay*." I told her not to be silly because if that had been so I would have called her *Bay-ah-tree-chay* right from the beginning. Anyway, after that I tried to be careful and not overdo it.

From my hospital bed I said, "*Bay-ah-tree-chay*, I'll buy you a new car. What kind do you want?" When she replied, "I *have* one that still runs fine," I probably shouldn't have tried to be funny. I shouldn't have said "Bea, you *had* one, but I wrecked it." But that was no reason for her to rub it in by asking, "Why on earth did you take my car? You haven't driven a car for years." Of course I haven't, but who needs a car in Manhattan? Besides, when we do need to go by car, she always drives. And who took off for Paris in the middle of the semester anyway? She or I? So I told her, "Bea, this is too long a story over the phone. I'll give you the details when I get home." "What do you mean, home?" she shot back. "Where are you now?" Only when she heard that I was still in the hospital did she sound concerned. I went on to say that the only reason I was still in the hospital was that I'd been knocked unconscious during the accident. They wanted to be sure I had nothing more serious than a broken left arm. This is when she came up with an extraordinary question. My wife of thirty-some years asked me—three thousand miles away in the hospital—whether I'd gotten the bumper stickers. But I'm jumping ahead of my own story. I always tell jokes this way—I give the punch line away too early. She first asked whether the front or the rear of the car got demolished. When I told her that it was mostly the front and the sides, she sounded relieved. Only then did she ask whether I had retrieved the bumper stickers. At first, I thought I didn't understand correctly, but when she spelled it out: "B-U-M-P-E-R S-T-I-C-K-E-R-S," I didn't know whether to laugh or get angry. Thank God I didn't laugh, because she really meant it. Instead I said, "Sure, I'll get your bumper stickers," but if I'd known what I'd gotten myself into, I would have kept my mouth shut.

I am supposed to be a leading Dante scholar—*Dantesoph* she called me when I had *Bay-ah-tree-chayed* her once too often. (It didn't help when I pointed out she was mixing Latin and Greek and that the correct term was *Dantist* or at times *Dantologist*.) Holder of the

Lamont Professorship in Italian at New York University; a man to whom cars are unnecessary burdens; who believes in supporting the taxi cab industry; and there I was heading for the biggest car dump in New Jersey. When we finally got there, I went up to the office, really just a shack, and asked the character in charge how I could get something from our Toyota. "What Toyota?" he asked. "The place is full of 'em." That was the first problem: Bea's car was a four-year-old Toyota—I never remember whether this makes it a '98 or '99—dark maroon, four doors, but I couldn't recall the model name. "When did they bring it here?" he continued as he opened some notebook. "I guess it was sometime during the last four days," I replied. After all, I hadn't made the arrangements, I had been in the hospital. And then came problem number two: "What's the license number?" he asked. The license number? How on earth would I know the license number? I don't burden my brain with such trivia. I don't even remember my social security number. Deliberately so. I'm not using up my available synapses for bureaucratic detritus that I can look up. I told him this in simple language—I figured *detritus* was not part of his vocabulary. The man gave me a look as if I were crazy. He slammed the notebook shut. "Find out your license plate number and then come back." I should've struck him dumb with "*Charon, bite back your spleen.*" But I doubt he'd read Canto III of the *Inferno*.

Instead of standing up to this car undertaker, this Cerberus of an automobile inferno, I shuffled back to the taxi, went home, and called my wife, forgetting that in Paris it was twelve thirty in the morning. "What's your car license number?" I asked. Actually, that isn't true. I felt foolish to start with this question. I tried to be amusing: "*Though I may come a bit late to my turn, may it not annoy you to pause and speak a while.*" I could hear her groan three thousand miles away. "Which goddam Canto is this?" "*Inferno* XXVII," I replied, but she didn't think it was funny or clever, not at twelve thirty a.m. So I got to the point: if she wanted me to get her bumper stickers, I first had to find the car, and for that I had to have the license number. And then I got another surprise. "DO IT," she said in a voice that had lost all drowsiness. At first I didn't understand. "Do what?" I asked. But then she explained that this is what our license plate said. "What do you mean, 'ours'? Yours!" I wanted to make it clear that in no way was I going to be associated with such a preposterous label. But how could it be possible that in two years of riding in the front passenger seat of her Toyota, I never noticed the license plate? I guess I never looked. What an asinine thing to put on a license plate. I wonder what she meant by DO IT? But then I had to admit that I hadn't even noticed that the car had any bumper stickers. "Do you know what your problem is?" asked my wife. "*Long promise and short observance. Inferno*, same Canto." If she hadn't hung up immediately, I would have shouted "*Brava*!"

I was still puzzled over how I'd managed to overlook the license plate. Do many people really know what's on their car license plates? I decided to perform as random an experiment as possible: I would question the first three colleagues that I bumped into at lunch at the faculty club. As luck would have it, my first victim turned out to be a philosopher, Jerome Scheldrich. He just guffawed. "Who owns a car in Manhattan?" was all he said. Noel Fenton was next. He immediately admitted that he didn't know the license plate number of his car, never had known it, and then—psychologist that he was—started to give me a detailed analysis of why he never remembered his own license plate. I just beamed. At this point I changed the rules of my private survey: when I saw one of my own colleagues, Mario Bonomico, at a table, I decided to ask him. A regular Italian, he turned out to be the most sympathetic subject. He did, in fact, know his license plate but only because of some heroic mnemonic device. He'd worked it out when his car was once towed away after he had blithely ignored a P.A. announcement about an illegally parked automobile with his license number. Somehow, I felt that the score was still 3–0 in my favor.

The next day I took another cab to the dump. I hate to think what I spent on these cab trips. If I had to have an accident, why, I ask, didn't I have it in Manhattan? Anyway, the same character was sitting at his desk. My God, I thought, *Inferno,* Canto V.

> There Minos sits, grinning, grotesque and hale.
> He examines each lost soul as it arrives
> and delivers his verdict with his coiling tail.

He recognized me right away. "Well, what's the license number?" he asked, in a pretty condescending manner. "DO IT," I almost shouted. "What ya mean, do it?" exclaimed Minos. "Do what?" I couldn't help laughing and then told him about the license plate. I guess that broke the ice; after looking in his book, he actually took me out into his empire. All I could think of was Cantos XXVII–XXX in the *Inferno.* Just as Dante made *the circuit of the pit*, seeing *torn bodies mangled and split open*, I stared at this incredible conglomeration of automobile carcasses. The man pointed in the general direction of the left fence and then departed with the words, "Your Toyota oughta be in there." While I stumbled around looking for a maroon wreck, two tow trucks arrived, one after another, to drop their smashed-up loads near me. So I dropped Dante and focused on this Jersey car dump. I had to be careful, with my arm in a cast, climbing around the wrecks. Finally I found DO IT—it was practically staring me in the face, but I was so overwhelmed by the mess that I had initially overlooked it.

And there were the bumper stickers. The print was small on the first one I saw and splattered with mud. Still I could make out part of the text: *Richest soil the soonest will grow wild.* Can you imagine, we drove around in a car saying this and I didn't even know it? There was a familiar ring about it, like a message in a Chinese fortune cookie, but what on earth was it supposed to mean on *her* rear bumper? I figured that I could work out the meaning when I got home. At this point all I wanted was to get out of the place with the bumper stickers. Then it struck me: I had forgotten to bring along a knife or razor blade. How was I going to detach the stickers? I went back to the shack to ask the man whether he could lend me a razor blade. "What for?" he asked, curiously eyeing my beard. When I explained to him that I wanted to remove some bumper stickers, he first looked puzzled and then, in a remarkably kind voice, provided a startling piece of information: "Razor blades make a mess. It's a cinch with a hair dryer." I was about to tell him that I do not usually travel to car dumps with hair dryers, but I resisted the temptation when I realized that his cooperation was worth more than a wisecrack. So I told the man that I might as well take the entire rear bumper and asked whether he would remove it for me. He gave me a sly look. "Sure, but it'll cost ya forty bucks." "Forty dollars!' I sputtered. "This is *my* car." "This *was* your car," he retorted. "We get them wrecks 'cause we store 'em here. If you wanna pay storage charges . . . lemme see, how long was your car here?" So I paid him. It was amazing how fast he got the bumper off, but you should have seen the face of the cab driver when the two of us arrived with a filthy bumper and asked him to put it in his trunk.

For once, I regretted living in a faculty apartment. I would gladly have dispensed with the subsidized rent in exchange for standard Manhattan apartment anonymity. In this place, you're not just apartment 9A, or the man in 14E. You're Jasper Ellis Duff from the Law School (why do these lawyers always spell out their middle names?) or Serge Goronsky from Math. These people know your departmental scuttlebutt before you even get home. That day was no exception. As I got into the elevator with the filthy bumper in my good arm, none other than Mrs. Basamutary, the nosiest person in the entire place, stepped in. "Professor Trippett," she asked before the door had even closed completely, "what are you doing with that object?" Thank God I was holding it so that the bumper stickers were facing my jacket. I just shrugged my shoulders and asked about her husband. Still, I am willing to bet that before that evening passed few people in the apartment building hadn't heard about Professor Lionel Trippett, of the Italian Department, clutching a dirty bumper in his right arm with his left one in a cast.

As soon as I entered our apartment I took the "object" into the bathtub and hosed it down. God, was it filthy! The bathtub was a mess, so I cleaned it while the bumper was drying. I then looked for a hair dryer. Of course there wasn't one. Bea had taken it to Paris. I was in no mood to go out again to buy one. I wondered where I could borrow a dryer in this apartment house without starting on a new list of questions. And then I remembered Professor Mitsuhashi, a new faculty member from Japan. His fractured English and that he was a chemist were sufficient grounds that our acquaintance had not progressed beyond the nodding stage. The Mitsuhashis turned out to be a good choice. When his wife opened the door, all I got was a startled "ah so" and the hair dryer. I wondered whether she ever told her husband about the *Grazie, bellissima* when I returned the dryer.

I sat down to inspect the stickers. There were three of them, all of uniform size, the print unusually small. One would have needed superb vision to read the fairly lengthy message from another car.

Now, of course, I had them within arm's length and, in addition, I wore my reading glasses. But as I cautiously aimed the hair dryer at the stickers and started to peel them off, I found another set of bumper stickers underneath them, and then a third layer. They had been glued on top of each other, rather carefully I must say, so that only three showed at any one time.

Suddenly I got goose pimples all over. The word *intellection* on one of the bumper stickers and the 3 by 3 theme had registered almost simultaneously. For Dante, 3 was the ultimate number: 3 parts to his Divine Comedy; 3 lines to each stanza—the classic *terza rima*; 33 Cantos for each part; 3 times 3, the magic number 9, to describe his Beatrice. But I bet that few people have ever heard of *intellection*, even though it's in the dictionary. However, it does occur in a couple of English versions of Dante—John Ciardi's and Mark Musa's translations of the *Divine Comedy*. Not in any of the others: Cary's, Binyon's, Singleton's, Sisson's, Carleye-Wicksteed's, Mandelbaum's, or Anderson's. I know all of them—that's my business. As a student I was brought up on the real classic—Francis Cary's—but Ciardi's is the most colloquial, in fact the only even faintly bumper-stickerish one. My Bea! My fantastic *Bay-ah-tree-chay*! I was so excited I spread the nine stickers out on the rug and numbered them: 1, 2, and 3 were the original three stickers that I uncovered last from the hair dryer treatment. Numbers 7, 8, and 9, of course, were chronologically the most recent. The one that I saw at the car dump turned out to be Bea's bumper canto number 8.

The Toyota Cantos

Burning logs, when poked, let fly a fountain of innumerable sparks.
I do not hide my heart from you.

The record may say much in little space.
Mortal imperfection . . . makes fit for intellection.

You seem to lack all knowledge of the present.
Why, when every lower sphere sounds the sweet symphony
of Paradise . . . there is no music here.

Why does your understanding stray so far from its own habit?

Portion out more wisely the time allotted us.

Lift your head. This is no time to be
shut up in your own thoughts.

Take care. Do not let go of me. Take care.
The taste of love grown wrathful is a bitterness.

Richest soil the soonest will grow wild
with bad seed and neglect.

Look at me well. I am she. I am Beatrice.
Losing me, all may perhaps be lost.

The time has come to make a confession: At that stage, all I had stumbled upon was the Dante numerology—admittedly a powerful key—and one word *intellection*, which turned out to be my Rosetta stone. I pounced again on Bea's nine bumper cantos—I rather liked the term and promptly made it part of my private vocabulary—to check for other Dante attributions. Portions of bumper cantos 1, 3, 8, and 9 turned out to be quite easy—especially number 9 ending with *I am Beatrice.* By now I was convinced that all had their Divine Comedy provenance.

At least three hours passed, in what proved to be a devilishly delicious game, before I woke up to the fact that I was doing precisely what Bea had been criticizing through her bumper *Tragica Commedia.* Clearly the point was to understand *what* she was saying, not *where* in Dante the quote could be found. I stopped looking for hints in the bumper cantos to Dante's Cantos. Instead, I reread them just for content and the message started to penetrate.

But let me return to my story. My new secretary's name is Jennifer. It's amazing how many young women in their middle twenties these days are called Jennifer. This Jennifer is one of the most efficient secretaries I've ever had. What's more, she's remarkably discreet. I figured she was precisely the person who could help me. "Jennifer," I said. (I never used "Jenny" or any other nickname with her, and I think that she appreciates it.) "Where can one order specially made bumper stickers?" This was likely to be a peculiar question for any man in his fifties, not just a professor of Italian literature. Nevertheless, Jennifer pretended as if this were the most natural question that could be presented to an academic secretary; especially one whose tasks deal largely with fourteenth-century affairs. Within minutes—thank God for the web—she produced the name of a place in SoHo that sold buttons, every kind of corny message, and lots of bumper stickers. She'd even confirmed by telephone that special orders could be filled within forty-eight hours.

The place was amazing. I must've browsed for a couple of hours when suddenly I found exactly what I needed. I only wished I'd thought of it myself. I still don't know why it was buried among the environmental texts: the whale preservation and no-nuke messages. I handed the slip of paper with the code number to the clerk. "Do you have this bumper sticker in stock, or do you have to print it?" I inquired. "Karma?" the man read. "Oh yeah, I get it. Where did you find that one? That's a new one on me. Lemme see if we have it." I stopped him. "Wait," I said. "Can you print that message for me but add a couple more words?"

I phoned Bea again in France that there was no reason for her to cancel her return flight—the arm in the cast didn't hurt any more, and luckily it was the left one. This gave me plenty of time to get the new bumper sticker and to ask Jennifer for a second personal favor. I'm not someone who uses his secretary for personal errands, but in this instance Jennifer understood why I needed her help. I wanted the old bumper to be highly polished—it was to serve as my new palette—and this was difficult to do with one arm in a cast. Furthermore, I wanted it wrapped in fancy gift paper with a large bow and I've always been a lousy wrapper of presents, even without a broken arm. But I didn't tell this to Jennifer.

Before I took the taxi to Kennedy airport to pick up Bea, I placed the long package on the coffee table with a big manila envelope on top of it. It contained the new Toyota sales receipt, the nine carefully dried and chronologically arranged old bumper stickers, and a brief letter. Writing it turned out to be a lot of work—much more than I bargained for—but Bea had set a precedent. It became my version of her bumper cantos, interspersed with some original Lionel Trippett.

"Oh my Beatrice, sweet and loving guide—"

I need not tell you where this opening comes from. At one time, it probably would have been typical of me to say that I am not "persuaded to give ear to arguments, whose force is not made clear." But in spite of this quote's origin (Par. XVII) it is unlikely to lead us to Paradise.

I could have answered: "The only fit reply to a fit request is silence and the fact" (Inf. XXIV) and added: "I have no recollection of ever having been estranged from you" (Pur. XXXIII).

I could have complained: "How sharp the sting of a small fault is to your sense" (Pur. III).

I could have equivocated: "Or have I missed your true intent and read some other there?" (Pur. VI).

But I am sure that you—who seem to have studied Dante in a way so different from mine—would have replied "the sense of what I wrote is plain, if you bring all your wits to bear upon it" (Pur. VI). Therefore, I have taken your advice: "Look deep. Look well" and Dante's (Pur. VIII): "If you seek truth, sharpen your eyes." Now that I understand "often, indeed, appearances give rise to groundless doubts in us, and false conclusions, the true cause being hidden from our eyes" (Pur. XXII), I promise: "I shall from now on no longer speak like one but half awake" (Pur. XXXIII).

If I "look closely now into that part of me . . . the part with which I see" (Par. XX), I realize that I took many things for granted. I was about to list these, but you should really hear them from my own mouth. You should question me; perhaps the way Dante was questioned before he was found to be deserving of paradise. I would like to do something that, strangely enough, we have never done in all our years of marriage: reading Dante together. Your "bumper cantos"—this is what I named your messages that, literally and figuratively, I never saw—showed me that there is at least one more way of reading the Divine Comedy. For once, I want to see it your way, because "the most blest condition is based on the act of seeing, not of love, love being the act that follows recognition." As you can imagine, this comes from Paradiso and I would like our joint reading to start with Canto XXVIII.

I cannot resist ending this letter with a line from Dante's very last Canto: "I feel my joy swell and my spirits warm."

I hope yours will too when you open the accompanying package.

Lionel

On the way back from Kennedy, I purposely refrained from talking about the accident or the car. I insisted that Bea tell me about her stay in Paris. It was the first time in years that she'd gone alone to Europe, so it was only natural that I'd be curious. I started getting nervous as we got into our elevator. Thank God, there was no Mrs. Basamutary, not even Mrs. Mitsuhashi. I led her straight into the living room and waited until she saw the package and envelope. "What's this?" she asked. "It's for you," I replied, "but first open the envelope." Bea gave me a curious look and then tore open the large, brown envelope. The sign of the old familiar bumper stickers produced a nervous laugh, which stopped as she started to read my letter. "Oh Lionel," she said in a totally unfamiliar tone, "you really don't have to . . ." "It's OK," I said. "Just open the package."

Carefully she opened the parcel, so as not to tear the wrapping paper. My wife is a compulsive saver of ribbons and paper—it drove me berserk at times to see her unwrap birthday presents. But this time, I didn't mind. I wanted everything to happen in slow motion.

"Oh, Lionel! Lionel, you nut, you didn't have to," she murmured. "You're repeating yourself, dear," I said and that's when she started to cry. She hadn't done so for years. Strange. After all, the only thing the new sticker said was

Your Karma Finally Drove Over My Dogma
(Lionel, *Purgatorio*, Canto Unico)

Author's Note

Prior appearance in somewhat modified form in the following publications is acknowledged: "How I Beat Coca-Cola" in the *South Dakota Review*; "Castor's Dilemma" in the *Hudson Review*; "Maskenfreiheit" in the *Crescent Review*; "Noblesse Oblige" (in German translation) in *Freundin*; "The Psomophile" (in German translation) in *Spiegel Spezial*; "What's Tatiana Troyanos Doing in Spartacus's Tent" in *Cosmopolitan* (U.K.); "The Toyota Cantos" in *Frank: An International Journal of Contemporary Writing and Art* (Paris).

Quotations from Dante's *Divine Comedy* in "The Toyota Cantos" are from John Ciardi's translation. Bumper sticker number 1 is from *Paradiso*, Canto XVII, and *Inferno*, Canto X; number 2 is from *Paradiso*, Cantos XIX and IV; number 3 is from *Inferno*, Canto X, and *Paradiso*, Canto XXI; number 4 is from *Inferno*, Canto XI; number 5 is from *Purgatorio*, Canto XXII; number 6 is from *Purgatorio*, Canto XII; number 7 is from *Purgatorio*, Cantos XVI and XXX; number 8 is from *Purgatorio*, Canto XXX; and number 9 is from *Purgatorio*, Canto XXX, and *Paradiso*, Canto II.

Photo by Karen Ostertag

Carl Djerassi, emeritus professor of chemistry at Stanford University, is one of only two living chemists to have been awarded both the National Medal of Science (for the first synthesis of a steroid oral contraceptive) and the National Medal of Technology. A member of the National Academy of Sciences, the American Academy of Arts and Sciences, and the Royal Society (London), he is also the recipient of thirty-one honorary doctorates and numerous other honors. He founded the Djerassi Resident Artists Program near San Francisco, which provides residencies and studio space for artists in the visual arts, literature, choreography, and music.

His literary writing (short stories, poems, five novels, eleven plays, as well as an autobiography and a memoir) focuses predominantly on themes related to science. His fiction and plays have been translated into twenty languages; several of his plays were also broadcast by the BBC World Service, the West German Rundfunk (WDR), National Public Radio (NPR), and other foreign broadcasting services.

Meet Carl Djerassi on the World Wide Web at www.djerassi.com.